TALES *from* TA'THALOON

TALES *from* TÀ'THALOON

CHRISTOPHER WOLFE

ACT I: AMBITION

Boyle
&
Dalton

Book Design & Production:
Boyle & Dalton
www.BoyleandDalton.com

Paperback ISBN: 978-1-63337-529-1
E-Book ISBN: 978-1-63337-530-7

Printed in the United States of America
1 3 5 7 9 10 8 6 4 2

This book is a representation of the efforts and support of many people. I am grateful to all those who have given of their time, energy, and talents. Without you, this book would never be.

ACT I
AMBITION

PROLOGUE

JALI PUSHED OPEN the door enough to peek over at her parents' room. It was dark. The only light came from a fire burning in the hearth of the living room, casting a warm glow over the thick rug and big comfy seats and illuminating the vase everyone hated and her mother loved.

A shallow cough resounded from the large chair nestled next to the fire. Would this be the last night they had together?

She wanted to say something, to do something. For years her grandfather had given the best of himself to help raise her and her brothers.

What would she say? Was there anything left to talk about?

"Jali," the ragged voice called. "Would you sit by me? Just for a moment or two?"

She shut her bedroom door quietly, listening to make sure her brother stayed asleep, and then she walked across the room and sat on the small chair beside her grandfather. He sat staring blindly into the glow. The orange reflected off his dulled eyes, but there was nothing wicked therein.

"It is late," he said.

"I couldn't sleep."

He shifted slowly in his chair and looked down into her eyes. Jali turned away. It was not embarrassment or shame that stirred her so. Her grandfather did not just look at someone, he *saw* them.

"Will you tell me a story?" she asked. "You used to tell me stories. When I was younger."

"Best to read a story. Time has not been kind to my memory."

"You remember breakfast every morning."

Her grandfather chuckled into a bout of coughing. "You have your father's tongue for which I suppose I have some blame."

"Jaja," she said. "I would like a story."

"Then I will tell you one. It is the first of many."

Jali reached out and took his hands. The skin was wrinkled and spotted with age. "How many?"

"Several. Separate but whole."

Jali thought about what her grandfather meant. "What kinds of tales? Will it be about a great queen? Like the ones you used to tell me?"

Her grandfather paused long enough for her to look up to make sure he hadn't fallen asleep.

"These stories are about people."

"Like you and me?"

"Just the same."

Jali frowned. "Jaja. No one wants to hear a story about me."

"I do. You are just as important as any queen." Her grandfather said this in a tone that told her it was not up for discussion. "Now, let's see what I can remember."

X

THE WEIGHT
OF SILVER

JATHALOR REACHED the top of the incline as night fell. High Town bustled with people. Lights covered every wall, and banners colored in bright, festive dyes hung in front of shops and between homes. He walked around and amidst people who were lost in bright smiles and endless giggles. He wanted to dance and laugh too.

In a courtyard to his right lay a long table filled with all sorts of strange food. His mouth watered as he wondered at the different flavors. Children, some who looked to be as old as him, were playing games and running with ribbons tied to sticks.

He stopped, got his bearings, and hurried to the left along the crowded sidewalk. He left the beauty of lights and headed into the large building that sat on the perimeter of High Town. There were no lights or banners here.

Jathalor dodged a man hauling a crate and moved to get in line behind the other workers. Pa told him that he didn't need to work, but he was almost eleven years old and strong enough

1

to help. One of the older boys said that festivals were a great time to work. Told him that people were in a better mood and he might even get a bit extra for working.

After a few shuffles into the warehouse, Jathalor peeked around the tall man in front of him.

Jathalor's boss, Havish, was a towering man with mostly gray hair and a pinched, angry face. Havish grabbed the shirt of the man in front of Jathalor. "Don't go making me get the whip! Get on with it."

Jathalor slunk back into line and took three deep breaths, trying not to think about when he had to face Havish. So much for people being in a better mood.

The warehouse they worked in was damp and chilly. The corners of the tall building were shrouded by darkness. Sometimes, the shadows convulsed. The people were mostly older than he was. They talked to each other in gruff sounds and quick sentences he didn't understand. Maybe there was a secret language that he needed to learn.

The tall man in front of Jathalor moved away, leaving him to face Havish. His boss shoved a box in Jathalor's arms. "Take this to the small shop across from Porter's Tavern. Ask for Karth. Be quick about it too. I've got more than a fair share of work today. Stars, I hate festivals."

Jathalor fumbled to get a good grip on the crate. His arms protested the weight. Jathalor balanced the crate on his leg before attempting to walk toward the door. His hand slipped.

"Careful," growled Havish. "The contents are worth more than a week's wages. Put your back into it and use the handles. That's what they are for. Hurry now."

Jathalor found the handles and tried to use his back. He took one wobbly step after another.

He managed to reach the door. Jathalor leaned onto the wall and propped the box between his leg and elbow to free one of his hands.

"Let me," said a calm voice behind him.

One of the other workers, a man about middle age, held his crate on his hip and used his free hand to open the door. "Don't worry," said the man. "It gets easier."

Jathalor managed a "thanks" as he wiggled his way through the door while grasping the crate.

He headed along the sidewalk, back into the midst of the celebration. A passing family of Katal walked in clothes of different colors. He didn't see a single patch, even on the boy's knees. The girl and boy were eating what looked like a piece of fruit covered in caramel and nuts. Jathalor felt his stomach rumble.

He adjusted his burden and walked on the far side of the street, in the shadow of the various shops and out of the way of the mob in the throes of celebration. The grand plaza of midtown was decorated with green boughs covered in silver and gold ribbons. In the center of everything stood a statue of the Katal's dead god, Naitharious. Rows of candles surrounded the icon.

Several musicians were playing and singing. In the far corner, a priest looked to be preaching to a gathered crowd. Children ran with sparkling sticks while adults sat and watched, drinking out of what looked like molded glass.

His fingers slipped out of one side of the crate. Jathalor leaned against the nearby wall and shook out his hand. The fingers were red and throbbing in pain. He gritted his teeth and wrapped his hand around the handle. Complaining did no good.

Jathalor continued his journey. It wasn't too far. Maybe Pa would let him join him on one of the ships soon. The pay wasn't any better, but Jathalor would rather be with Pa.

The crate slipped again. He steadied it. His shoulders and lower back were starting to hurt. Jathalor breathed in and out. *I can do this.* He wished his Pa was here to help him. Pa always seemed to know how to work and never once complained even though his back hurt often and his feet were battered and bruised. Jathalor gritted his teeth. He'd grow up to be good, just like Pa.

"Let me help." The voice came from a tall woman wearing nice clothing. She balanced a tray of drinks in one hand as if it were nothing at all. "Set it down."

Jathalor carefully lowered the crate to the ground. He couldn't let anything happen to the contents. Havish was an angry man.

"Take a moment to breathe. You are no use broken."

He was standing on a sidewalk near a garden with tall bushes for walls, some in pots that were shaped strangely. Men and women wearing expensive-looking clothing were talking, drinking, and forcing smiles at each other.

The woman moved the tray low enough for a short, fat Katal to grab one of the glasses of crimson liquid. She made it look so easy.

"A drink and a show," said the man, looking at the woman in a way that made Jathalor feel uncomfortable even though he wasn't sure why. "Shame you're not Katal."

Jathalor couldn't tell if the woman was Camoor or not. All adults looked the same to him. Especially in the fine clothing, she might've passed as someone celebrating. Of course, she wouldn't be carrying drinks for anyone if she wasn't working.

The woman seemed unbothered. She gave Jathalor a reassuring smile. "Now. I want you to squat down and grab both sides. That's right. Lift your head and look straight ahead. You are going to lift with your legs and keep steady with your back. Are you ready?"

Jathalor lifted with just his legs. Keeping his head up was harder than he thought it would be. The woman placed a hand on his back.

"Use your legs. Too much back," she said. "That's better." She held his back until he was standing.

Jathalor grimaced when he felt the weight tugging on his arms.

The woman moved the tray so that a passing Katal could grab one of the glasses. She gave Jathalor an apologetic look. "You're so young. Chin up. It gets better."

"Thank you," Jathalor told her, and he wanted her to know he meant it.

She merged into the crowd. Jathalor continued his labors. It was easier. Still hard, but he could manage.

Jathalor reached Porter's Tavern. The three-story building stood at the edge of one of the largest streets of High Town. The windows were open, and he could hear music and the raucous sounds of people drinking. There was even a crowd gathered outside the tavern.

He maneuvered his way through the mess of bodies and across the street. There was only one shop with its door open. What was the name of the man? He struggled to remember what Havish had told him. Havish would want him to be quick so he could get back to help move more crates. What was the name?

"Karth?" Jathalor blurted out, using his leg to hold up the crate as he blundered into the room.

The small, cramped room was filled with men smoking pipes and drinking out of short, squat-shaped glass. None of them even looked in his direction, but why should they? This was the kind of place only Katal lounged. Porter's Tavern was open to all. Not here; only Karth cared, and his concern was with the contents of the crate.

He wandered farther in, trying to summon the courage to call out again. There were all sorts of strange smells and most of them only worth wrinkling his nose at. On a shelf behind a large counter were rows of weirdly shaped bottles containing different colored liquids. One of the men at a nearby table breathed out a long drag of white smoke that ballooned before vanishing into nothing.

Jathalor remembered his work, mostly because of the weight on his arms and back. "Karth?"

A hand grabbed his shoulder. "Voice down," said a boy. He looked to be only a bit older than Jathalor. A bruise under the boy's left eye was colored yellow and black. Motioning to the crate, the boy asked, "Is this from Havish?"

Jathalor nodded. The boy grabbed one side of the crate. "This way."

Jathalor nearly laughed out loud when they started walking. It was so much easier with help.

"Aromor."

"Jathalor."

"Good to know you."

"Same."

They maneuvered through the crowded shop and headed to the far back. Several haggard-looking men sat smoking and drinking. There were cards, dice, and coins scattered across the table. It was more money than Jathalor had ever seen.

"From Havish?" asked one of the men. The man, probably Karth, was round about the face and stomach with meaty arms and a thinning head of brown hair. He rose from his seat and grabbed the crate.

Karth heaved it with ease to the side of the room onto a squat table. He pried open the top of the crate.

"That's not the point," Karth said, turning to face the other men. He grabbed one of the bottles while he was looking in the other direction. "You and I both know it's not as simple a matter."

Jathalor picked at the loose string next to the hole in his pants. What if something had broken on the way? He hadn't been as careful as he wanted to be, but it was so heavy.

One of the men grumbled something Jathalor didn't understand. Karth turned back to the crate and checked the contents with a scrutinizing gaze and deft fingers. "Mark my words, something is brewing. I'd bet good money we're only a few years from war." He picked up one of the bottles. "Oh ho!"

Jathalor's heart sank into the pit of his stomach. Something had broken.

Karth held the bottle out for the table to see. "It must be the holidays. Havish never lets me have the good stuff."

Jathalor waited for the rebuke. The boy working for Karth probably got the black eye from doing something wrong.

Karth put the bottle back, grabbed a piece of paper, and scrawled something on it. He turned to Jathalor, who cringed.

It only hurts at first. Time heals pain. The reminders didn't actually help.

"Boy," Karth grumbled, shoving the paper at him. "There's work to be done."

Jathalor took the page from Karth.

"That's my promise. You can tell Havish I won't send this much silver with an errand boy. He'll understand just fine. This," Karth produced a silver coin with the queen's face on it, a half dollar, "is for you."

Jathalor held both hands out. The Katal casually dropped the coin into Jathalor's palm. "You'll need to go to Darran's next. He's a few blocks down."

Jathalor stared at the coin. He wouldn't have believed it was real if he didn't feel the metal pressed against his skin. More than a week's wages.

"Boy!"

Jathalor slipped the silver into his pocket and pressed his hand over it.

Karth handed Jathalor an even bigger crate. "I need this delivered to Darran."

Jathalor took the crate, his back screaming in protest at the weight.

"And boy, don't spend that silver all in one place. Maybe shoes, or a shirt." Karth looked over Jathalor with obvious disgust. "Anything, really."

Jathalor struggled under the weight of the crate but headed back into the shop with resolve to do a good job. He could buy good food. Or maybe one of the delicious-looking fruit sticks. He should save it for something better than a treat.

The crate slipped through his fingers. Jathalor caught it, set it down, and got ready to lift it like he was supposed to.

"Out of the way," said a man, bumping into Jathalor.

Jathalor waited until no one was close and got ready to lift. Aromor grabbed one side.

"Come on," Aromor said.

Jathalor and the other boy lifted the crate. Together they navigated through the shop and out into the street.

"We need to hurry," said the boy. "Karth doesn't want me leaving during shift."

"You can't get in trouble. Not on account of me."

"This is too heavy for you. No offense or nothing. Katal don't think enough. They—" He refrained from saying more. "Besides, I've got a talent for getting in trouble."

They headed down the street out of the way of the throng of celebrators. A loud chime sounded from the towering chapel to the east. Everyone around them cheered and raised their hats or glasses.

"This will be tricky," said Aromor.

Jathalor held on with both hands as they cut across the street, around and in between the raucous crowd. Someone bumped into him. Jathalor nearly lost hold of the crate. They waded deeper into the chaotic mess of people.

Elbows and shoulders jostled him constantly. He shifted his grip while he tried to keep pace. His knee kept nudging the crate. He almost ran into one of the Katal but stumbled to the side instead. Somehow, they made it out of the mess and onto the other side of the street.

"This is the place. Darran don't mind much. Just look for a tall, bald Katal." Aromor held the crate out for Jathalor.

Jathalor fished in his pocket for the silver. He pinched it between two fingers. His own personal fortune. Pa always talked about people being who they were and not what they had. Aromor had gone out of his way to help.

"Thanks," Jathalor told him, leaving the coin in his pocket.

"I'm needing to get back." Aromor held the crate out for Jathalor to take. "Hope the rest is good."

"Same to you," said Jathalor, taking the handle.

Jathalor watched his friend leave, guilt twisting in his gut. Just a coin. More than he'd ever had, but still nothing worth more than another person.

He felt his back start to protest the weight, and his thoughts snapped to an angry Havish calling for the whip. He lumbered into the shop. Men mingled below clouds of smoke and boisterous conversation.

"Over here," called a voice.

Jathalor headed over to the bald man, Darran, sitting toward the back. There were three other Katal at the table and they were arguing about something. But it didn't seem like they were mad. Just loud.

Jathalor waited just beside Darran. He felt his arms starting to tremble from the weight.

"No," said Darran. "War makes a profit for a few but—"

"That's my point," one of the others said. "I'm not saying it's good or right. Forbid we talk about justice. I'm saying it makes sense because a few men profit—"

"You're telling me members of a Bureau from Nestali would be stupid enough to start a war for a few coins?" asked Darran. The man leaned back in his chair and tapped the table. "Listen here. The Bureau may be witless fools, but I've known a few of the Ministers of Defense. They've enough problems without trying to start a war."

The crate kept getting heavier for Jathalor, but he breathed through the pain and kept his focus on making sure he didn't drop it. He felt his sweat-greased fingers giving way.

"Boy. What are you doing? Just set it over there." Darran pointed to a stack of similar crates behind him.

Jathalor waddled over and set the crate down beside the others.

"Not on the ground," grumbled Darran. He got out of his chair and stood. Darran was taller than most Katal, broad-shouldered with fierce eyebrows. The lack of hair anywhere else probably made them seem bigger than they were. But they were bushy eyebrows.

Jathalor stood waiting for the rebuke.

Darran rubbed his right knee and looked intently at Jathalor. "Oh," he muttered. "You ain't from Karth, are you? Nope. Bet you one of Havish's. Karth told you to tote that over anyway."

Jathalor kept silent, not sure if he should say anything. He did need to get back.

"Listen here," said Darran. He lifted the crate onto one of the others with ease. "Havish won't have you being late, and you already are. You might as well make a bit of coin before going back. I'll have you run something for me."

Jathalor cringed at the thought of carrying another box. At least if he headed back to Havish he could rest before the next delivery. Maybe the silver would be enough to keep Havish from doling out too rough a punishment.

Stars, not the lash. He scolded himself for cursing. Pa'd be mad. "I really should—"

"Boy," Darran said sternly. "I wasn't asking."

Jathalor hung his head and waited for the burden. Darran's footsteps sounded as if they led farther into the shop where he seemed to rummage for a bit.

"It's not far," said Darran. He held out a small crate.

Jathalor took the burden. It was so light.

"Head down three streets until you hit the corner of Main and Garden."

"Boy can't read," someone said from behind them.

Jathalor looked up at Darran. "He's right."

Darran frowned. "Suppose I need to do a bit of thinking. Oh, I know. I have a page with the symbol on it. One of their advertisements, I think." He got something from inside a desk and brought it back. "Head out the door, take a right, and go until you see a group of wagons with this picture. Bunch of travelers come here for the holidays is all. You're looking for a woman. She's real pretty, black hair, and she's got herself a bracelet. Silver maybe. Can't quite remember her name. You'll know her. And boy, take this."

Jathalor watched Darran place a silver coin on the crate. "That's for your troubles, and this—" he placed a small bottle inside the crate, "is for Havish. Tell that dog I wish him warm holidays."

The table of men chuckled. Jathalor's head swam with a mixture of excitement and fear at the thought of facing Havish. Then he thought about Aromor. Now he had two coins. He should've shared.

"Thank—"

"No time for that. There's work to be done." Darran pushed him in the direction of the door.

Jathalor headed outside and took a right. He wasn't struggling to breathe with each step. The world felt brand new. He
watched people dancing, laughing, and chatting.

He paused at the end of the street and watched as a procession of horses and people wearing costumes paraded by. He
continued once the last group of colorful celebrants cleared. As
he passed by the open doors of the church, he heard the throng
of voices all singing some hymn. Beautiful stained-glass windows, alight by candle flame, covered every wall of the towering
building. He wanted to know what it was like inside, but he
wasn't allowed.

Festivity and excitement whirled around him in so many
colors, sounds, and smells that he almost forgot he was working.
Jathalor glanced down at the page. The picture contained several
words and a large symbol that looked like the sun. He would be
able to find it. Hopefully.

Jathalor reached the end of the street and looked around.
Standing on top of a small stage, playing a stringed instru-
ment, was the most beautiful woman in the world. He steadied
the crate as it slipped out of his fingers. His gaze drifted back
to the singer.

Her hair was gold like the sun. Her skin was as fair as snow
in winter. She sang and it made him feel as if everything in all the
world needed to stop and listen.

The crowd around her listened. Katal entranced by a
Camoor. What a strange moment. She looked so confident. So
sure. Jathalor listened to the steady pluck of the strings and her
angelic voice.

The song ended and he found himself wishing it hadn't.

I need to get back to work. It was a sad truth that he'd listen to. He wanted to stay to hear if there would be more. There was something about music he didn't fully understand and didn't want to. He loved it for what it was and what it meant to him. Before Ma passed, she used to sing to herself when she was out cleaning clothes or working in the garden. Maybe she didn't think anyone was listening, but Jathalor always was.

Jathalor tore himself away from the singer and swore he'd learn her name if only to remember the moment better.

He glanced down at the page to make sure he knew the colors and symbols correctly. He looked up in time to see someone walking right into him.

Jathalor wrapped his arms around the crate as he fell to the ground. He hit with a hollow thud and a soft crack.

"Boy," shouted the man in a crisp, demeaning voice. The man's face was pinched tight like he was trying hard to think about something. He was taller than most men and wore robes decorated with embroidery of gold and silver. Rings carrying gemstones of stranger colors covered most of the man's fingers.

Jathalor might have marveled at the fortune on the man's hands if he didn't have to think about the crate and the broken contents.

A bullish-looking man with thick arms and a mean face stepped right in front of Jathalor. "Should I teach him a lesson?"

A tall, slender woman with thin lips, also wearing robes, walked around Jathalor. She only had one ring on. "Kalliom, call off your hound. We do not have time for this intrusion. Not when we are so close."

The two people in robes walked into the crowd. The mean-looking man stepped on Jathalor's fingers as he passed. The crunch of bone against stone ground in Jathalor's ears. He felt tears starting to well in his eyes, but it wasn't for the pain of his bleeding fingers or throbbing elbow. He had failed.

"Come now," said a voice, stern and soft. The speaker was a man, young in face with honest eyes. He knelt and grabbed Jathalor under the arm. "Best medicine for a fall is to get up." The stranger produced a rag and wrapped Jathalor's fingers with a steady hand.

"Braeron," called the robed man.

"I'll catch up," Braeron shouted. "Wretches. All of them."

Braeron helped Jathalor to his feet and looked him square in the eyes. "You remind me of my brother. You've some determination. No need for tears. Pain is just a part of living. A reminder we're still alive." He looked past Jathalor. "Stars. I need to catch them. Be good." And just like that he vanished into the crowd.

Jathalor stood, hand throbbing. His right pant leg was ripped, and the skin on his knee was torn and bleeding. He clung to the crate and checked the picture, but there was no page.

He searched around him, frantically looking under feet and around people, but the picture was gone. *How will I find it now?* He stopped, chest heaving, knee bleeding and mind racing over what he should do.

Before him, painted onto the side of a large wooden wagon, was a symbol much like a sun. Several men and women were gathered.

Jathalor looked around for the woman. What had Darran said about her? Dark hair and a bracelet of sorts? There were several dark-haired women in the crowd and many of them were wearing jewelry.

There. He didn't even need to second-guess. The moment Jathalor saw her he knew that she was the one he was supposed to be meeting.

Shame haunted his steps as he walked toward her. He couldn't explain it, but disappointing this woman felt worse than being late for Havish. Besides, he still had the bottle to give to Havish. What if that had been broken?

Jathalor felt on the verge of tears as he approached the woman. She was lounging on several cushions next to one of the wagons. Jathalor still thought the singer was prettier than she was, but she was beautiful. On her wrist was a bracelet consisting of three separate pieces all linked together. The bands were covered in strange script.

She introduced herself, but Jathalor couldn't remember the name or pronounce it. He smiled politely and presented the crate.

"Oh, from Darran. What a kind-hearted man." She opened the crate and handed the lid to someone nearby. "Some of my favorites. What a wonderful gift, just in time for the holidays."

Jathalor stammered to say something about the bottle for Havish and an apology for the broken bottles. But none of them were even cracked. He was sure something had broken in the fall.

"This," she said, pulling out the exact bottle Jathalor was worried about, "must be for Havish. You work for him? A pity." She shrugged and handed him the bottle. "But, a Camoor needs to eat."

Jathalor took the small bottle. She told him about their company, and then he was leaving. It was all a little fuzzy, but she gave him two silver coins for his trouble.

Four in one night, a fortune. The reality made him giddy

with excitement, and sad that he hadn't shared with Aromor.

Then he remembered Havish. Jathalor hurried along the street and took the alley behind Darran's shop. If he jumped the fence a few streets down, it should put him closer to Havish's. There was probably still plenty of work to be done.

He headed into the dimly lit alley. His pocket made a soft clink with each step. He loved the way it sounded.

"That's a lovely sound." The speaker emerged from the shadows. There were two of them. Rough-looking Camoor. Jathalor saw the marks on their arms just below the elbow. Gang members.

Jathalor turned and walked quickly back the way he came. Then he ran. He listened as the footsteps behind him grew louder and louder.

One of them shoved him forward. He landed on his bloody knee, twisted over, and smacked his elbow. The piercing pain screamed a warning. *Cover your head, let them hit your legs and arms.*

"What is going on here?" called a voice.

Jathalor looked at the stranger, hoping for a Law Keeper and finding a middle-aged man wearing nice clothing. A Katal. His stomach sank.

"Nothing to worry about," one of the ruffians said. "Just a bit of a talk between Camoor."

They pulled Jathalor into a seated position. One of the gang members gripped Jathalor's shoulder so tightly it started to hurt. He stifled a whimper.

"Looks to me like a robbery," the Katal said.

"Might be. What's it to you? We can share whatever we find—if that's what you're after."

Jathalor wanted to plead for help, but what Katal would care about him? Even a Law Keeper might turn their head for a price.

"Let him go," said the Katal.

"This is *our* business. You've no reason to bother, hear me?"

"You are right. It is just a Camoor, after all."

Jathalor lowered his head and prepared for the beating.

He felt the grip on his shoulder loosen suddenly. The Katal threw the thug against the alley wall and slugged the second ruffian in the face. The gang members fell limply to the ground.

"Scum," the Katal grumbled. He walked over to the thug struggling to recover from his recent meeting with the wall and lifted him off the ground by the throat. "Your kind has no place in Nathalem. I have a word or two for the Briars, specifically your boss. Tell him Taf sends his greetings."

The Katal dropped the gang member. The mangy Camoor struggled to breathe as he limped away. The second thug lay cold on the stones. Was he even still alive?

"Best to keep to the streets and out of the shadows," Taf said, looking down at Jathalor. "Especially during a festival."

Jathalor nodded enthusiastically. He tried to say thank you but couldn't manage the words.

"What is a boy of your age doing out so late?" Taf's eyes narrowed on him.

"I've work to do," Jathalor sputtered.

"So young," said Taf. "A shame, but a Camoor needs to eat. I cannot escort you back to work, for my own labors keep me. Promise me you will keep to safer routes."

"I promise." Jathalor reached for a silver in his pocket and produced it. "Thank you."

Taf smiled, and it felt genuine. "A generous gift, but I have no desire to take it from you. It is an honor to serve and protect you."

"I've more than I need," said Jathalor, putting the coin in Taf's hand. Should've shared already. "I owe you my life."

"I would see you safe." Taf picked up the coin and held it out for Jathalor.

Jathalor hurried back toward the street.

All the way back he kept one hand on his pocket and the other grasping the bottle for Havish. Jathalor rehearsed several lines of apologies. He needed to explain the work for each man. Karth and then Darran. What was the woman's name again?

He reached the warehouse and headed inside. Havish was screaming at someone for something. Jathalor steadied his nerves as best he could and hurried over to the desk. When he saw Havish's face as red as a ripe tomato, he considered just going home and looking for new work. But it wasn't easy to find a steady job.

Please, not the lash. Jathalor waited until Havish finished berating his last lackey before he popped into view.

"Depths take you, where have you been?" growled Havish. "I'm behind several deliveries because of you. Did you take a nap? This will be coming out of your pay. For the week, mind you."

None of Jathalor's rehearsed lines made sense anymore. He stammered something unintelligible as Havish snatched the bottle and peered at it. "Darran, that old dog."

"Warm holidays," Jathalor blurted.

Havish looked at him with a frown.

"It's what master Darran told me to tell you."

Jathalor waited for Havish to call for his whip. Maybe it would just be a backhand. Either way, he just wanted it done so he could finish work for the night. Stars above, he wanted some sleep.

"Warm holidays indeed. Listen here. Don't you be taking any more jobs from those louts. You work for me, do you understand?"

"Of course, master Havish."

Havish pulled open his desk. He fished out a silver coin and tossed it over to Jathalor. "Take the rest of the night, but I expect you tomorrow."

Jathalor stared at the coin.

"Get on then, boy. I've got work to do."

BETTER LEFT DEAD

AN ALIEN GRINDING echoed off the ancient, crumbling walls of the tomb. Kalliom took a step back. He needed to find Cai'Tallai's final resting place. The missing research would be the final piece to a puzzle Kalliom had spent his entire life working on. The noise started anew.

"That can't be good," said Catear. The Katal had trunks for arms and a thick neck with a small head and beady eyes. He was prone to red cheeks. Thankfully, he was not paid to pontificate.

"Oh really?" Braeron asked. The younger Katal came highly recommended. He boasted twenty years of age but looked to be only seventeen, especially with the stubble he called a beard. There was some reassurance in knowing he knew who to sacrifice first if events turned unfavorable.

The grinding noise grew in volume until Kalliom could barely hear his own thoughts. A loud thud exploded in front of them, sending bits of rock and dirt everywhere. Kalliom somehow managed to keep his feet although he felt his legs protesting the sudden shift in weight.

I need to get out more, he told himself. Years of working inside with stacks of books had left him devoid of some of his natural vigor. There was a time when he could have left for days and still be ready for more adventuring.

Catear and Braeron both held their lanterns revealing a large bolder now blocking the way into the tomb.

"That's really not good," said Catear.

"I hope we never find ourselves at the mercy of actually needing these coinswords," said Haili. The Thow was younger than him with only one ring of master. She had decided to come along mainly because he promised her it would provide an interesting break from her normal studies while fulfilling a requirement for one of her current masteries.

Her face caught the light of the nearby lantern. She wore her blond hair back, but a strand constantly fell in front of her ear. She was always pulling it back. He found himself thinking of her as pretty.

Kalliom had difficulty admitting it, but he was growing fond of her. Of course, she was intelligent, but there was a craftiness to her that most Thow missed. She knew how to apply what she learned.

Kalliom watched as the two Katal argued about the new roadblock. "I would not worry yourself over the matter. Consider them to be insurance."

"How sure are you that this is the tomb?"

"She has been correct thus far." *Although I find myself in doubt.*

"Is this a personal contact or a professional one?"

That was an interesting question to ask. Perhaps she did not just come along for the discovery. He saw her in a new light, and there was nothing distasteful in what he could see.

"Professional, strictly so. We have mutual interest in this project."

A loud, annoying grinding grated against his ears. Kalliom held his head and turned away from the sound. The noise ended in a loud boom.

The boulder was gone. Debris flittered down from the ceiling."

"Perhaps it would be best if we did not activate the trap again," Kalliom pointed out.

Catear held his hands up. His fingers were like sausages. "How else we getting to that door? You yourself said it needs opening."

Kalliom leaned over to Haili. "You are right. I hope we do not need them."

He enjoyed her chuckle and remembered that he was still responsible for getting past the door. No one else would have a mind to solve the problem.

Braeron jumped forward. Kalliom waited for the boulder to crush the foolish Katal, but he remained disappointed.

"What's this?" Catear asked.

Braeron threw out his hands. "Hold. Don't go making a mess. I'd rather not be jam."

Catear stood close enough to the where the trap had triggered to make Kalliom take a step back.

Braeron jumped as if he were playing some child's game. He moved across the floor until he reached the door. He seemed to be choosing his place carefully although Kalliom could see no differentiation to determine the reasoning. His aged eyes did him no favors.

Kalliom heard more rumbling and stepped back, holding Haili's arm and coaxing her to join him. She did not seem bothered.

A loud boom echoed down the hall. Dust and debris scattered. The door was open. Kalliom felt a sudden ease. His contact would not suffer failure, and he had no desire to find out how she would deal with disappointment.

"I don't know if the trap—" Braeron started.

Catear walked toward the door.

Kalliom waited, but nothing happened. One step closer to finding Cai'Tallai's tomb. He was not sure what would be waiting for him. The master was renowned for many discoveries, but it was his later interests that were Kalliom's concerns. If this tomb contained what he thought it did, the world would never be the same. The next great step in evolution.

Braeron held his lantern up, the orange eating through the darkness. Kalliom walked toward the doorway, studying the floor and seeing what he could not see before. Patterns etched into the floor, faded but visible. He moved to get a better view of what lay behind the door.

A rib cage lay pinned to the doorframe with a massive glaive shoved through the chest cavity. Kalliom wandered closer and examined the weapon and bones. Just inside the tunnel, the rest of the skeleton lay in a scattered heap. Kalliom eyed the weapon. Something about it lured him closer, despite fear and the darkness beyond.

Majestic craftsmanship, the entire weapon was made of the same metal from top to bottom. The massive blade at the top looked to be heavy enough to compare with a guillotine. The rest of the weapon was suspended from the wall. The back end of the weapon was honed to a sharpened point. The longer he stared, the more he was convinced the metal gave off a soft blue glow.

"This belonged to a king among kings." Haili stepped forward and leaned closer to the blade.

"No one going to ask the question needs to be asked," grumbled Catear.

Kalliom looked over at the Katal. "And what is that?"

"What kind of man can wield such a weapon?"

It was actually a wise question, and maybe that was why it annoyed Kalliom so much. He glanced over at Braeron and motioned him into the recently exposed tunnel. "Check for any traps, and see if you can find out what kind of beast is responsible for this."

Braeron stood still, his lantern already poised to cut into the darkness beyond. He breathed out before heading into the tunnel. Kalliom felt a sickening desire rise in his stomach. What he wanted most was to hear a deafening cry and the sound of some trap making an end to Braeron's life.

Kalliom contented himself by studying the weapon and skeleton. He reached into his pack, took a piece of paper in both hands, and gently pressed it against the blade's edge. A sharp slicing sound accompanied the page being neatly severed.

"What kind of metal can keep an edge after all these years?" asked Kalliom.

"The kind we can sell for a fortune." Catear stood over the glaive with obvious greed in his eyes.

"If you can remove it from the stone, I believe you are more than entitled to sell it." Kalliom turned around and looked to see if Braeron's light still shone. It was there, the orange hue unmistakable in the dark.

Kalliom left his fear behind and ventured forward. He

glanced behind to see Catear grabbing the massive glaive. Even the mighty Katal's greatest effort ended in frustrated curses, but the Katal tried again.

The tunnels looked no different than the ones from before. Lifeless gray with few variations. Kalliom knew better than to assume that a tomb would be anything more, but this was the resting place of one of the greatest Thows of all time. Kalliom certainly felt entitled to expect something.

They joined Braeron, who stood with his lantern held high. The tunnel ended at a door unlike anything they had seen so far. There was nowhere else to go. Either this was Cai'Tallai's tomb or this was yet another wasted trip.

The door was made of polished black marble, the frame hewed from stone. A large, circular symbol covered the upper half. It looked to be interlocking pieces of gold set directly into the black marble. If he were to guess the design, it was mimicked after the brain with a phrase inscribed across the middle. *The Master of Minds*. It was what Cai'Tallai called himself in several of his last publications.

"Beautiful," said Haili, stepping up to the door.

Kalliom turned to Braeron. "Did you find any traps?"

Braeron shook his head. "None that I can find. To be honest, I am more worried about what awaits inside."

"It has been centuries since these tombs have been explored." Kalliom stepped forward and touched the door. "We have certainly made it past the worst."

The marble did not seem to want to budge. Just like the last door, there was no clear handle or latch. Just the slight protrusion of the symbols. Kalliom tested the gold to see if it shifted or twisted, but the metal did not budge.

Without Catear nearby to say anything stupid, the three of them stood in silence. Kalliom started to grow frustrated as the countless possibilities he constructed in his mind resolved with absolutely no answers. He did not come all this way to be stumped by a door.

"Did you check around the frame?" Kalliom asked Braeron.

"Checked the walls too."

Kalliom crossed his arms. "We will get Catear to break it down."

Braeron chuckled. "He'd try."

Haili stepped up to the door and touched the symbol. "Perhaps the lock is more obvious than we think."

"I already tried to move the symbol. It is stuck fast."

Despite his proclamation, Haili started to test the various pieces of the metallic symbol. Part of the symbol shifted away from the rest and slid to the side before stopping with a click.

"Interesting." Kalliom stepped forward and looked at the symbol's variations with a newfound curiosity. Each section seemed to be a part of a bigger mechanism. He thought it was just one large piece of metalwork, but it was obviously interconnected.

Haili shifted more pieces until they hit another roadblock. Nothing else on the symbol moved. Could it be that easy? Kalliom eagerly waited for the door to start opening. It never did.

"Do they come off?" asked Braeron.

The Katal stepped forward and worked one of the pieces back and forth. The golden chunk of metal slipped free of the door, leaving a notable gap in the symbol and a slight impression in the marble. Kalliom stepped forward. He placed a hand on the next section and tested its flexibility. With just a bit of force, the piece slid away from the rest.

"The real question remains," said Kalliom. "What kind of puzzle are we dealing with?"

Braeron held the lantern while Kalliom and Haili took all the pieces off the door, leaving an indentation.

Catear joined them just as the pieces were set on the ground. The massive Katal leaned against the wall, chest rising and falling. "Is that it?" No one mentioned anything about his failure to remove the glaive or the foolishness of his belabored attempts, but no one had to. His face said it all.

Kalliom kept his eyes focused on the pieces neatly arranged between Haili and him. "For now. Once we get this door open, we will find out what real treasures this tomb has to offer."

Catear bobbed his head. "About time for some real treasure."

Kalliom and Haili started to organize the pieces, fifteen in all. With them spread across the floor, he could almost imagine that there was some sort of pattern. At first glance he would have guessed that the pieces were part of a children's game. Most were either square or rectangular in shape with a few being rounded along one side. He could easily balance them on top of each other or construct a house of sorts with them.

Time matured curiosity into frustration. Braeron and Catear hunkered down farther in the hallway, killing time playing with dice. Haili glanced between her puzzle and her journal. She kept an intricate log of the events with notes dating back to their first conversations about Cai'Tallai. Another impressive characteristic.

Kalliom shifted his weight and felt his legs protest. He leaned to the side, resting his weight on one haunch before forcing himself to the other side.

"I need to walk," he grumbled, struggling to get to his feet as his legs protested the sudden movement.

Kalliom paced down the length of the hall, feeling better with each step. Catear and Braeron grumbled and cursed as he stepped over their game of dice. From what he could tell, Catear was winning. That surprised him.

He reached the fallen door and studied the glaive. Despite all of Catear's attempts, the weapon remained deeply embedded in the stone. How many men did he know who were stronger than the monstrous Katal? He counted one, and even that man was only slightly more of a brute than Catear. A Vyrasar might be able to, and that was a history conveniently unwritten.

Kalliom leaned over and examined the blade. The metal looked too much like steel for him to guess what its base element was. Was it possible that the ore had been refined even further until it became so dense that it was impossible to break? Well, nothing was impossible to break.

He paced back and forth, over the game of dice and around Haili's continued attempts at solving the puzzle. He always respected her work, but he wondered if this was a question without an answer. What they needed was a key. Perhaps a lexicon to clarify what the symbols meant, and from there they could determine if a message or a phrase would be used to open each door. Was there an entry from one of the journals that would provide the information they needed?

Kalliom paced back toward where they came from, stopped in front of the open door, and stared at the jutting glaive. Before, he had imagined the weapon belonged to a defender of the tunnel, but what if it was someone trying to escape? The blade fit so snugly in the stone it almost looked like a massive key.

The two Katal shouted after Kalliom as he ran past them toward the dim light of Haili's torch.

"We are looking at it the wrong way." Kalliom got down on his knees and picked up two of the pieces. "We need a key."

Haili glanced between her journal and the pieces. "But the door does not have a place for a key."

Kalliom ignored the logic. He set the two pieces aside and started to test the stones one by one. The first few refused to connect on any level. Further attempts came with the same frustration. Excitement faded as the idea proved impossible.

He grabbed another piece and lined up the symbols. "Useless," he grumbled, pushing out a huff of frustration. The two stones slid into each other with a satisfying click. The symbols ran together, each of the lines connecting perfectly. Haili looked up from her journal. They shared an excited expression.

Kalliom quickly started to piece the puzzle together. Haili joined him, bracing and holding the metal when it proved necessary. With every addition, the conglomeration of stones went from a disjointed mass of fragmented pieces to a single entity. The runes no longer appeared to be random.

The last piece of metal clicked onto the edge of a box with a perfect circle on one side. Kalliom grabbed the edge and strained to lift the metal. He quickly gave up and turned toward the Katal.

"Catear, make yourself useful."

Catear walked over and handed his lantern to Haili.

Kalliom approached the door and pointed at the symbol. "I believe that is the top. Place the symbol onto the door."

Catear frowned as he lifted the metal into place.

"Thought this was the door?"

Kalliom watched the metal fit into the indentation.

Catear pushed the symbol in but quickly adjusted his hold. "Braeron, a hand."

Braeron held one side while Catear braced on the opposite end. Kalliom picked at his nails as they pushed and twisted the symbol. Finally, with the circle facing the door, the metal box clicked into place on the door.

Kalliom held his smile, waiting for the door to swing open and his years of searching to finally be validated. Nothing happened. The metal box was just stuck to the door.

"What if there is another puzzle?" asked Haili.

Kalliom clenched his fist. He almost shouted, but Catear interrupted before he could say anything.

"It is still a door," said the massive Katal, pushing on the stone. "Even I know that."

The doorway groaned and shook as Catear braced against the door, pushing with both arms and legs. A distinct thud echoed off the walls. Catear looked back at Kalliom.

"Told you," Catear said, and pushed the door open.

Kalliom hurried into the room. After years of searching, he had finally found it.

Rows of dusty tomes covered a shelf to the left. A massive desk sat in the corner, holding more untold treasures. Across the room was a sarcophagus.

He stopped when he noticed the statue towering in the middle of the room. It was a head taller than most Katal, arms thicker than even Catear's, with heavy plate armor covering every inch of it. Kalliom might have missed the most disturbing revelation if

31

Braeron had not come in and raised his torch high. The neck of the statue was flesh, gray and lifeless with thick black veins visible through the nearly translucent skin.

The statue twitched. Kalliom took a step back as the monstrosity's head moved. The thick plating of the helmet stopped. Empty white eyes fixated on Kalliom. The statue took a step forward.

Kalliom twisted around and ran out the door. Haili followed him into the hallway, leaving the two coinswords behind. Catear stood with his mace and shield at the ready, facing the giant with the courage of an unchained lion while Braeron, sword in hand, looked more like a mouse.

Kalliom could not count the number of times he'd seen Catear fight over the years. Obviously, the Katal had yet to lose.

"Best to move on," Kalliom shouted at Catear. "See if we can lock the beast in its cage again."

The statue slid a sword free with a slow, steady motion which produced an ear-grating scraping. Kalliom could not be sure, but the sword seemed to gleam like the metal from the glaive.

"Cower all you want," said Catear. "This is just another door in my way. Don't take my light away though, I hate fighting blind."

The statue, beast, whatever it was, swung at Catear. The attack was painfully slow, as if the mass was actually made of stone. Catear side-stepped and smashed his hammer down on the statue's face. The metal did not bend. Once, twice, and a third time Catear struck the helmet.

"May want to drop the tunnel on it," Catear told them.

Kalliom wondered if there was a substance they could use to melt the metal.

Catear continued to dance around the enemy's attacks, testing different parts of the armor for weakness. It might have been amusing if Kalliom wasn't constantly worried that something of importance might get crushed or damaged in the process. He did not want any of the research ruined.

Haili turned to Kalliom. "We could conduct research while Catear and Braeron take turns keeping the beast preoccupied."

"Not a bad solution." Kalliom watched Catear back into the desk. The aged wood creaked and groaned.

"Careful!" Kalliom shouted.

The Katal ducked under the next swing and moved inside the monstrosity's guard. He grabbed the helmet with both hands and attempted to pry it free.

"This thing is just muscle and steel," shouted Catear. "I don't know if there is a way to break through."

Kalliom stepped into the room and examined the doorframe. He still had no idea how to close the door. Maybe they could lure the statue into the hallway before conducting their research.

"Do not trouble yourself about winning this fight," said Kalliom.

"What else am I to do?" Catear grumbled. "Should I just dance until we are done?"

"That is the idea."

Catear stepped back, eyes watching the monstrosity as it methodically stepped toward him. "Not likely. The longer we fight, the faster it gets. Going to be an actual problem soon."

"We will do what we can before then."

The statue stepped forward and swung, twice as fast as the last time. Catear caught the attack on the shield. The statue's sword sunk deep into the reinforced steel as if it were butter.

Catear stumbled backward, losing his footing but managing to stay upright. The Katal scrambled to pry the pieces of his broken shield off his arm.

"Stars!" Catear shouted. "What kind of demon is this?"

Kalliom watched the movements of the statue carefully. He realized that all the other work in the room paled in comparison to this contraption of flesh and metal. Here was Cai'Tallai's greatest achievement. A monster of flesh and metal who had survived for how many years?

Catear gripped his hammer with two hands and let out a feral roar. The Katal raised the weapon above his head and brought it down. The metal smashed into the armored forearm of the statue and rebounded backward. Catear took his own hammer to the face.

Kalliom stopped breathing. Catear fell backwards, landing on his back with a lifeless thud. Kalliom watched for a rise or fall of the man's chest. Braeron grabbed Catear's arm. The statue stepped onto Catear. Braeron pulled, but the heavily armored foot broke Catear's chest with a gut-churning crunch.

"We need a new plan," said Braeron, dropping the limp arm.

Kalliom put a hand over his mouth to keep from gagging. Haili stood frozen, her eyes on Catear's broken body.

"Best we move," Kalliom told Haili, putting a hand on her shoulder.

Braeron hurried out of the room and stumbled after them as they headed down the hall. They stopped. The sound of the monstrosity's footsteps echoed off the walls.

Kalliom thought about Catear's chest. *No*, he scolded himself. Progress required sacrifice. It was a lesson history taught time and time again.

Braeron glanced back. "Time to retreat."

Kalliom shook his head. "Nonsense. We have come this far."

Haili grabbed onto his arm. "We may not ever leave if we do not take our chance."

Kalliom looked over at Braeron. "You were hired to defend and protect us. I certainly hope you are still up to the task."

Braeron turned in the direction of the statue as it stepped into the hallway. The shrouded figure loomed larger than Kalliom remembered. It stepped forward and the cave trembled. Maybe they did need to leave.

"You know," said Braeron. "If Catear hadn't been a fool, this would be easy." The Katal looked over at Kalliom. "If I live, I'm taking Catear's pay. You can double mine. "

Kalliom chuckled. "Right."

"I'll just go."

"This is a terrible time to negotiate. We can talk about this after. When we're not dead."

Braeron smiled, his confidence unsettling. "Or I'll leave."

Kalliom gritted his teeth. Odds were the Katal was going to get himself killed anyway. "Fine. Enough gold to drown your petty life in ale."

"Because that's all coinswords do." Braeron set everything he had on him aside, including his weapons. "I'll dance with the monster. Head into the room when an opening presents itself." Braeron took off his leather chest piece and shirt. "Don't be taking too long. I've a feeling this monster isn't long from waking up."

The monstrosity was already almost halfway to them.

Braeron tightened the straps on his boots and belt. He watched the advancing enemy. Maybe he would not die right away. What really mattered was having enough time to get some research done. If it came down to it, he would have to sacrifice Haili and take her notes with him. That would be a shame.

Braeron hoisted his torch high and walked toward the statue. The Katal stopped. The statue raised its weapon and swung. The speed was almost as fast as a normal soldier's attack.

Braeron stumbled backward, the weapon scraping the wall and leaving a gash where it struck. "Stars," the Katal said, backing away. "This isn't going to work."

The statue advanced and swung again. Braeron dodged under the attack. Another dance, faster but just as deadly, started. Braeron stepped backward. Sweat glistened on his head and back. Kalliom guessed they might have at most one pass down the hall before Braeron made a mistake and paid for it.

Braeron rolled into the next attack and came up on the other side of the statue. The statue advanced farther toward them, ignoring the coinsword. Kalliom stepped backwards.

"Braeron," he called.

"Working on it."

Haili stepped back, holding the lantern. "I do not know if this is worth our lives, Kalliom. Not mine, anyway."

Kalliom put a hand on her back. "Come now. Sacrifices are a part of discovery. You know this."

Braeron struck the statue's back. Metal ground against itself as the monstrosity struggled to reach around. It took a step to the side and then another toward Braeron. It followed the Katal down the hall until both figures were swallowed by darkness.

"Now, Kalliom," said Haili. "We need to leave now."

A harsh echo resounded from the darkness. Kalliom

swallowed and stepped back. Braeron was dead and they were next.

But the sounds did not come any closer. Kalliom stepped forward, curiosity swallowing every measure of fear. The footsteps fluctuated. Back and forth.

The noise grew louder. Kalliom watched as Braeron, panting and sweating, came into view of their torchlight.

The Katal huffed. "Go," he sputtered. "Hurry."

The statue came into view, advancing with sword ready. Braeron ducked and side-stepped as the blade sliced to the right, putting a notch in the wall.

"Come on!" shouted Braeron. "Finish me!"

The statue advanced with sword raised and swung down. The blade sunk deep into the stones. Braeron moved behind the statue. The monstrosity turned around and swung at the Katal.

What is he doing? Kalliom retreated far enough back to be safe, past the first door.

Braeron came around the statue and started to run toward Kalliom. "Back," he said breathlessly, waving a hand.

Kalliom slowly moved backward. He picked up the pace when he saw the statue start to run toward them. It was as fast as a man, covering a huge distance with each stride.

Braeron stopped a few passes from the doorway, shoulders rising and falling with each breath. He was bleeding from several places.

"Here," the Katal said. "Come on. Finish me!"

The monstrosity charged at Braeron with sword raised. Braeron dropped and rolled backward. The statue ran into the protruding glaive. Metal scraped against metal in a deafening screech. Braeron scrambled away as the sword left the hands of the monstrosity and fell, sinking into the floor below the glaive.

Braeron crouched in the doorway, poised like a cat ready to pounce.

The statue twitched. The glaive's shaft jutted out of the creature's back.

"Is it dead?" asked Haili. She stepped forward, casting her light over the monstrosity.

"The real question is, was it ever alive?" Kalliom stepped forward and examined the portions of flesh and metal he could see clearly.

Braeron rose to his feet and leaned against the wall. "I know you're worried, but I'll be fine. Right as a new day."

Haili stepped forward, the light shifting with her. Kalliom moved so that he could get a better view of the monstrosity's face. Gray skin, resembling his own with a touch of decay, was seemingly fused directly with the metal. Kalliom had never seen or heard of anything like it before.

Haili looked over. "I think I will go find what can be found in the room. Braeron, perhaps you could do something about Catear. I would rather not trip over the dead while I work."

Braeron looked between the two of them. "You've had me dance with demons and won't lend me time for a breath?" The Katal stood up. "If it weren't for the King's Bounty I'll be taking with me, I'd leave you all in this corner of the depths. Don't know how I'll tell my mother about this."

Kalliom watched the two of them leave but settled himself where he was. Haili was right to go and see what knowledge the room held, but Kalliom knew that Cai'Tallai's greatest achievement was this masterpiece of flesh and metal. Before it was over, Kalliom would learn how to replicate the process.

His mind caught on an odd thought. His source had been correct about the tomb and what he would find, and yet she didn't ask for payment or credit for the discovery. All she wanted was for him to continue his research. Everyone always wanted something. Whatever she was to gain from the process would no doubt be costly, but this was his life's work. Over twenty years of dedicated research culminated in a discovery that would shape the future of Ta'Thaloon.

Kalliom admired the amalgamation of flesh and metal. "Together, you and I will change the future."

A KNIFE FIT
FOR A KING

TAF STOPPED. He checked down either side of the hallway, all the while listening carefully for anything out of the ordinary. Satisfied, he opened the door and stepped inside. He turned the lock until it clicked shut.

"An assassination attempt is planned for tonight," Taf said, looking at the gathered few. They were all veterans. Two Law Keepers and Arma, a member of the King's Shield. "Lathu and Boran, I need you on exits and entrances. This gathering is small with no direct outside connections, which means we are dealing with a traitor."

It did not escape Taf that one of the men working security that night could well be the assassin. He had kept his insight secret for that very reason and handpicked these men. Boran had the King's ear which was rare for one so young. He was clean-shaven with his hair kept short.

"How do we know?" asked Lathu. Unlike Boran, Lathu wore his sandy blond hair long. He also allowed a small patch of fur to grow on his top lip. It was fashionable and distasteful.

"I listen to stories of shadows," Taf said. That seemed to be enough to reassure the two Law Keepers of the severity of their responsibility.

"Do we have anyone tasting?" asked Arma. The other member of the King's Shield was younger than most, but one of the best fighters and strategists Taf knew. He was clean-cut with a shaven face and a calculating expression.

"I have safeguards in place. Leave the details to me." Taf had assigned the chief taster to check every plate before it reached the King. Everyone else thought he was out because of a head cold.

"Is there anything specific we are looking for?" asked Boran.

Taf crossed his arms. "We know it is happening tonight. I do not know who is behind the threat. We assume it is a Sythari contract. The information did not come easily."

"Stars above," cursed Lathu. "Never even seen a Sythari. What should I be looking for?"

"Sythari operate quickly," Arma said. "They are obvious assassins. Look high, low, or out of sight."

Taf nodded solemnly. "Obvious maybe, but quick and effective. We need Law Keepers and guards both on high alert. I would keep the rotations often but do not draw unwanted attention. If there is a rat in the crowd, I would rather burn him out before he, or she, can get away."

Boran turned to Lathu. "I'll get the second and first floors on a rotation. I promised them a training exercise soon. We can make it seem like this is an exam the Chief asked for."

Lathu nodded. "I'll make sure we don't leave any glaring gaps as we shuffle."

Taf leaned over and whispered to Arma, "Take first leave. I will be downstairs eventually."

"King and Kingdom," Arma said.

"King and Kingdom," repeated Taf.

Taf interrupted the Law Keepers. "Do you both understand your additional responsibilities?"

They both nodded and went back to their hurried discussion. It was reassuring to see a measure of zeal. Perhaps he had made the proper selection.

The Law Keepers left after a few more moments of hurried planning. Taf mulled over his plan, adding a few additional contingencies. Tonight was supposed to be a casual celebration of a minor victory in securing some new policy connected to the Church of Naitharious coinciding with some coming-of-age ceremony for the King's son. Which meant priests and nobles in plenty. Taf reached inside his tunic and felt the handle of his blade. *I would rather be on a battlefield.*

He slipped out of the room, closed the door, and walked down the hallway toward the nearest water room. Castle Victory was adorned with banners of white decorated in various styles of purple and gold. A collection of musicians entertained the crowd in the main hall below. Three entrances and exits plus two secret ones.

The floor above him was the personal quarters of the royal family. There were mosaics on the ceiling of the great hall. The three skylights created a potential vantage point for a skilled archer, such as a Sythari, but the King would never be moving to a place with a clear shot. One less contingency to plan for.

Taf entered the water room and used the polished stone to check his recently shaved face. He adjusted the button on his cloak until he was satisfied with the way the cloth rolled over his right shoulder. The tunic was in good order with the crest of his position polished and carefully pinned over his left breast. His belt was tight enough to keep everything together.

The face that looked back at him was older than he remembered. The few gray hairs he had plucked over the years were only useless attempts to stall the inevitable. Now, he could not even begin to count the number of silver stands mixed into his dark brown.

Clearing his throat, he listened to make sure no one else was in the room before he headed to the back, through the supply closet, and pushed in the stone that unlocked the secret stairway. Taf closed the wall behind him as he went down.

He exited the stairway into a small cove connected to one of the reading rooms on the first floor. Once he was sure no one was nearby, he pushed open the bookshelf and shut it silently. He slid his favorite book off the shelf and took a seat on one of the cushions.

Outside, the commotion of the crowd was hearty but subdued into the quiet murmur associated with highbrow gatherings. *Ugh. Small talk.* In his life he had faced impossible odds on the battlefield, torture, and numerous life-threatening injuries. Nothing prepared him for parties.

Taf flipped open the book to where the middle of the pages were cut out. Inside was a small parchment.

The Shadows had found something useful. He took a random book off the shelf and sat himself in the corner. He dabbed a cloth with a special oil that smelled awful. Using the book to hold the page, he dabbed at the parchment until the words revealed themselves.

The dying speak. Duplicisis. What did a constellation have to do with an assassination attempt?

The phrase left by the Shadows meant that the person they captured and learned the assassination attempt from died with this word on his, or her, mouth. It could be the word used to start the assassination, a piece of lingo used by the group, or the garbled nonsense of a tortured mind about to pass.

He sighed, got up, and walked over to the bookshelf. Sliding both books back into place, he popped the scroll into his mouth and swallowed. It caught in his throat, so he worked it down with saliva and determination.

Taf reached into his pocket to grab his small talk cheat sheet. His fingers bumped into the silver coin, and his thoughts drifted to the dirty, bleeding boy in the alley. *I vowed to protect.* He resolved himself to brave nobility. Still, he checked over the various details about nobles and priests he had stashed for this very occasion.

He headed into the gathered throng with a confident posture. A passing waiter handed him a glass of wine. The crystal was the finest in the Kingdom and, from what he heard from the serving staff, a pain to clean and polish.

He checked over the various details about nobles and priests he had stashed for this very occasion, and resolved himself to brave the party.

The first group of noblemen he approached included an old friend. Taf reached out a hand to Lord Tavean. The graying nobleman eagerly exchanged a hearty handshake.

"Taf, or should I say 'Fist of the King,'" said Tavean. "It has been some years."

"Taf. Unless you want me to address you as 'lord' every other breath."

"Stars, no." Tavean gave the others in his group a polite gesture and motioned for Taf to walk with him. "You look well enough. Did you finally find a woman to keep you honest?"

Taf did a quick check to make sure guards were all at their stations. "Believe me when I say the title is more than just a fancy name to throw around parties. My time is spoken for."

"Come now, plenty of men in your position have found a means to balance both. What about that woman? Oh, what was her name. Maisi?"

Maisali. "She did not appreciate the fact that my time was spoken for."

"You are not getting any younger, my friend. Do you at least take time for company? I would not judge a man for keeping his bed warm."

Bed was for sleeping when the work was done. "You know how it is. Lonely nights are best shared."

"That's the truth."

Taf worked to remember what he knew about Tavean. He could recount the exact routes someone could take to get into the room. "Tell me, how is your son? The last time we spoke you said he was considering the faith?"

Tavean laughed. "It has been some years. My son may have considered the faith, but that was as far as his pursuits took him."

Taf mingled until he found an opening to say farewell. He endured two more rounds of meet and greet before slipping off into the outer rooms. He checked on several guardsmen he knew personally and introduced himself to a relatively new recruit.

Lathu was standing at the edge of the hall, just out of sight and right where he was supposed to be. The King was in the midst of a toast. After the speech, he would move to the ballroom. This was the second most critical window of the night.

Taf turned into the room and maneuvered through the crowd, checking a few spots to make sure the right people were in place. The King started to move. Lords and ladies of the court drank and chatted in a blur of disregard and fake laughs. Taf kept pace with the King's movement, always where he could see the junctures where someone might rush in with a knife. The transition to the ballroom was uneventful.

Unfortunately, he needed to pretend he was not occupied only with the King's safety. Begrudgingly, he moved back into the crowd. After he checked his sheet.

Three nobles later, he shook hands with a Lord Dutha. Taf had known Dutha's father well. A well-spoken nobleman who had spent decades helping to reform and refine the mess that was Nathalem's public affairs policy.

"Fist of the King," said Lord Dutha.

"Taf is just as well. Better, in fact."

The woman hanging onto Dutha's arm was distractingly beautiful. Her light hair fell about a revealing dress. The most intriguing part about the woman was the intricate silver bracelet on her left arm. Were all three bands interconnected?

Dutha introduced her, but Taf struggled to remember her name, much like every one of the other lords and ladies. Too many so-and-so's.

"We were just discussing how we would approach war," said Dutha.

The crowd of nobles were a part of the younger generation. Not one of them had done anything substantial in court, at least to his knowledge, and several sported unbecoming mustaches.

"A light subject," Taf said, sipping on his diluted wine. "Perfect for parties."

"We need to be ready," said one of the lords. He looked young enough to be Taf's son. "You cannot deny that tension between east and west is worse than it has ever been."

Taf finished the glass of wine and set it on a tray that was passing by. "I will need a few more drinks before I start giving away all my secrets."

Dutha interjected with a tone and pitch similar to the one Taf had heard from Dutha's father so many times in court. Stern and confident. "We need no secrets. War is inevitable. Three hundred years of peace is longer than any of our fathers imagined."

"You sound resolved."

"As he says," said the young, mouthy noble, "it is inevitable. Better to be prepared than ignorant."

Dutha nodded. "It is a fair point he makes. My father often told me that life is filled with hard decisions, but it is up to those with authority to make them."

Taf was sure that was not the end of what Dutha's father had told him.

"Which is why we need to consider how drafting will work," said a different noble. The pale-faced man looked confident as he addressed a subject that meant death and life. "Of course, the Camoor population should be the first to be drafted."

The group of men nodded their agreement.

"And why is that?" Taf asked.

"Losing a few Camoor is inconsequential. It might even cut back on the King's taxation of nobles. We are the means by which they live, after all," Dutha pointed out.

Taf tightened his fist. It was a bad idea to argue with nobles. *I should not.* "We are? Tell me, lord, when was the last time you spent time in Low Town?"

"Why would I bother going to Low Town? It is dirty and of no significance."

The mouthy noble chimed in with a distinguished air of snobbery. "Low Town is a drain on the crown. Tell me if I am wrong. Because I am not. Every year most of the coal used to keep that pit from freezing over is supplied by the King. We are taxed to ensure that the labor happens, and that provides jobs for the Camoor. The whole system works in their favor."

Taf could tell them of the numerous Camoor he knew by name who worked day and night to provide basic needs for their families while these wretches rotted in their opulence. He wanted to explain that their hard work provided the foundation by which these nobles enjoyed their snobbery. Without toil, the soil bears no bread.

"I suppose it is worth reminding you that if the Founder's River freezes, all of Nathalem would be covered in ice for the whole winter." Taf faced Dutha. "I believe this conversation has concluded. Lord Dutha, you have a legacy to protect. Do not forget what your father lived for."

Taf stole one final glance at the woman attending Lord Dutha. It was not her beauty that haunted him. There was something else.

"Fist of the King," said Lord Dutha, bowing respectfully. "Thank you for your time."

Taf left the group, catching a few of the next words spoken. If those men were Nathalem's future…he tried not to think about the ramifications.

He mingled with one last nobleman before checking each of the entrances to the ballroom. Everyone was in place. New rotations were happening without any obvious issues. *If I were the assassin.* His thoughts stopped abruptly.

Lathu and Boran were sitting on a set of chairs near the corner of the room. Both men were lying back in their seats with glasses in hand. Taf swallowed his anger and assumptions.

"I take it the party is finding you both well?" Taf asked. He placed a hand on the back of Lathu's chair. Out of the corner of his eye, he saw his knuckles turning white.

Lathu hung his head.

"Sir," said Boran. "I assure you that everything is in accord." His words stumbled over each other.

"Did I make a poor choice?"

Lathu set his glass aside. "We should ensure rotations are flawless."

"Right," Boran muttered.

Taf let go of the chair. He tried to correct where the fabric was starting to rip. Nothing he did helped. *Stars.* He breathed out. Nothing had happened to the King yet, the room was secure. Still, they should know better. Boran was not even one to drink, not like Lathu.

He headed opposite the two Law Keepers. Lords and ladies began to dance as the band played more familiar tunes.

Taf wondered if he still knew the steps. Maisali and he used to be rather good.

Taf shoved all those thoughts aside. Time and circumstance had thwarted his chance at love. He was thankful enough for purpose.

A soft whistle called his attention. Taf ignored it, continued walking and grabbed a glass from a nearby tray. He rounded a table, gave a few old acquaintances his regards and headed toward the back of the room.

Arma walked past him, dropping something into Taf's hand as they passed. Taf slipped the small rock into his pocket.

Taf waded through the crowd, found an opening, and headed into the nearest water room. Once he was sure no one was around, he pulled the stone out. White engraving with one dot. The castle was secure, and Arma wanted to meet at the eastern tower soon.

Taf slipped the stone back into his pocket where it clanked against the coin and picked a route through the crowd. He shook hands with a few lords before using the servants' alley to avoid a large cluster of younger nobles, including Lord Dutha. He could just hit the boy. His father had always been so concerned for the Camoor. For equality.

"Taf?"

The voice was enough to make Taf's heart stop. He locked eyes with the most beautiful sight in the whole world.

"Maisali?"

She strolled over to him wearing a regal dress of dark purple embroidered with gold. It was as if she had not aged a day. Taf stopped himself from reaching up to check his hair. *Is my shirt tucked in?*

"It has been some years," she said, holding a hand out for him.

"We are older," said Taf, kissing the top of her hand. "I mean to say—"

"I know what you mean. You are right. It has been too long."

Taf instinctively held out his arm for her. She took it and they walked away from the crowds and onto the patio. They took residence on the left side, by the railing overlooking the road down to Low Town. It was where they always went during ceremonies to escape the cluster of snobbery.

"You look well."

"Tavean made the same comment. Does everyone think I am incapable of taking care of myself?"

"Well," she asked. "Are you?"

Taf looked deep into her brown eyes. There were specks of green and gold. For a heartbeat, he forgot. Everything. Reality crashed back in with the terrible thought that she might be married. He never called or wrote.

"I manage." Taf looked away, putting both hands on the railing, and breathing to steady his heart. It did not help.

"Without help?"

"Without help."

They stood in silence for a long time. Taf mustered what courage he could find.

"I owe you an apology?"

"This should be fun," Maisali said. "Is this a current confession, or are we going down memory lane?"

Taf rolled his eyes. "You never did let me off easy."

"You never let yourself breathe."

"There is no time for that."

"There never was enough time."

Taf's thoughts stumbled over each other as he scrambled to find words. His heart twisted inside of his chest. "I did what I could. I know it was never enough. It was not a decision I wanted to make."

"We never made a decision."

"I am sorry I never wrote. Or called on you. Stars." He leaned farther into the railing. "I was in Eastwatch two years ago. For almost a week, and I never even called."

"I know. I kept waiting."

Taf pushed off the railing and turned to face her. His affection for her raged like a storm within him. How did he ever let her go?

Behind them the guards on the patio changed. The King was going to move soon. Taf had to be ready. There might be an assassination tonight. He did not have time for old affections.

"I need to go," he said.

"You always did."

Taf took one step forward and stopped. "I would have given you the stars if I could have. You are the most wonderful woman. Forgive me for never being enough."

He felt like he was one step behind himself as he walked his carefully planned route. He even talked and laughed with an old friend, but every second felt disjointed. There was so much more he wanted to say to Maisali. *I should write.*

The King started to process out of the ballroom. Taf took up his location and kept in pace with the King. Everything transitioned perfectly. The whole group entered the throne room without incident.

Taf left it all behind and headed toward the eastern tower, realizing for the first time how much the distraction had cost him. *I cannot write.* His job was to serve the King and he could not afford distractions on a night such as this. Better to be done with the affection. The pain he felt was cold and deep, but he thought it was right.

Arma was waiting for him at the top of the tower, looking out a small window that gave a great view of the castle grounds. "Both transitions have been without issue."

"It has been a quiet night." Taf leaned on the wall opposite Arma. "Forgive me my tardiness."

"You should have taken more time."

"It cannot be afforded. Not tonight."

Arma turned to face him. "I checked behind both Law Keepers. They did an excellent job organizing the guard."

"It does not excuse their actions."

Arma shrugged. "This is a party. What high-ranking Law Keeper does not enjoy themselves at these events? I wondered what you were doing when you choose Lathu. Do not mistake me. He has a brilliant mind. It is simply wasted. We need to get to our places."

They started to walk down the stairs. Taf had spent a significant amount of time thinking about every detail of the evening. Why did he chose Lathu?

"Why did you not marry Lady Maisali?" asked Arma.

"What gives you the notion we ever considered marriage?"

"Everyone assumed as much. The whole court spoke about it for months."

Taf did not have a good answer. "She was given a place at the court of Eastwatch. Besides, I had little time to give. There was no marriage to be had."

"Was that her opinion, or yours?"

"Two nights when I am not traveling is not a marriage. She deserves more."

"In matters of the heart, two nights may be better than none at all."

Taf stopped, two stairs from the bottom. "I serve the Crown, first and foremost. Being the King's Fist only means more responsibility."

"When I was serving in the north I was married. We saw each other only as often as I was not somewhere fighting some border scuffle. It was not what some may think of as ideal, but it was good for a time—"

"And then it ended."

"Yes," said Arma.

"Further to my point."

"Because she passed."

Taf felt every part the fool. "Forgive me. A poor assumption."

"There is no need for apologies. I remember doubting it would work. Have you taken the time to listen to what she would say?"

"The past is in the past," Taf told him. It was as much for himself as anything. "I am going to run a sweep of the west."

Arma waited by the door. "I have the east. Only a bit longer now. It has been quiet."

Taf took a path through the serving quarters to reach the western end. *Maybe I should talk with her.* Would she even care to discuss it now? It seemed like a different life.

"Sir," said Lathu.

"You are supposed to be overseeing the Royal Guard."

"I have Jotho currently in my position. He was your chosen replacement for Boran."

Taf felt his neck burn. "And where is Boran? Enjoying the party?"

Lathu did not meet Taf's gaze. "He was unable to enjoy his enjoyment. If you take my meaning."

"So he is indisposed. Wonderful. I am to be the fool for this evening."

"Sir," Lathu stuttered. "There has been no incident so far. Boran's behavior needs to be corrected, but the Crown is safe."

Taf unclenched his fist. "Life comes and goes in the blink of an eye. The well-being of the eastern realm is dependent on the King. Little do people know all he does for the Kingdom."

"I understand the responsibility. I only mean to assure you all is still in order."

"As it should be."

"Sir," said Lathu. "I know it may not be my place, but perhaps it might be a good time to call on Lady Maisali."

Taf crossed his arms. "Is the whole court privy to my past affections?"

"You left your post to speak with her. I only assumed there was a reason. The King does not move for some time. You would be suffering no failure to take some time for yourself. The King may not know all you do for the Kingdom, but others are not so blind."

"I want the entrances checked again," said Taf. He walked past the Law Keeper and headed into the crowd to find Maisali.

How could he be so foolish to choose Boran for this evening?

Would Maisali still want to discuss anything with him? This party was turning into a mess.

As his heart rate slowed enough for him not to feel the thump in his neck, he mulled over the twisted thoughts crowding his mind. The guards were well structured. Arma was doing his part well. He should have asked if he knew anything about Duplicisis. Maisali would tell him exactly what the clue meant if he had taken the time to ask her. Lathu was right. He needed to talk with Maisali, if only to keep his attention from being pulled in different directions.

The best of friends makes the best of enemies.

The line was from a well-known play Maisali had made him attend more of than he liked. A story about Duplicisis. Taf stopped walking. His mind gathered the distorted fragments of the evening and sorted through the chaos. *Lathu.*

Taf causally shifted his walk and headed right for the throne. He drew his dagger. He lifted his arm enough to let the blade slip into his sleeve and kept it out of sight but within reach by holding the pommel against his thumb joint.

Boran was a man from good stock who never drank. Lathu remained sober all evening. There were only a few reasons a man abstains. Taf shoved and pushed his way through the throng of nobles. If Boran was unable to do his part, Lathu would take his place. Boran was supposed to be nearest to the King.

The King was seated at his throne, and where was Lathu positioned now?

"Shield the King!" bellowed Taf.

Royal Guardsmen ascended the platform where the King sat. The room churned with muttered voices and the heavy thud of hurrying boots.

Taf shoved past the last few nobles. He leapt onto the landing and started running.

Lathu moved into position next to the King.

"Your majesty," Taf shouted. "Mind your head."

The knife held in Lathu's hand struck the throne where the King's neck had just been. Two Royal Guards grappled the weapon free of the traitor's grasp before pinning him to the ground.

"Move the crown and secure the room." Taf stopped in front of the wriggling Lathu. He looked to one of the Royal Guardsmen. "Boran should be somewhere on this floor. He may be hurt or worse."

Taf turned around. Lord Dutha stood in front of him with a knife held to strike. Taf let his blade slide into his palm, but he was not fast enough.

A sword flashed in front of Taf and disarmed the assassin. Taf raised his dagger to the traitor's throat. He turned the man around and held the blade carefully against the jugular.

"There may be more," Taf said.

Arma was already searching the room. "We will have any other traitors found. Forgive my oversight. I should have known Lathu was involved."

"Ashes all. Crowns to rust." Lord Dutha started to tremble. "Ashes all. Crowns to rust."

Taf struggled to hold the man. Blood started to spurt onto his hand. The madman was trying to kill himself. Taf adjusted to keep the traitor from cutting too deep.

"Ashes all. Crowns to rust."

"Arma," Taf grunted. "Shut him up."

"Ashes all. Crowns to rust. Watch the skies. Gray to tell the coming night." The traitor lunged forward into the knife. He tumbled to the ground, blood spurting from the gash in his neck.

Taf watched the man's eyes roll back in his head. There was a bit of foam around his mouth.

Arma stood next to Taf, sword at his side. "Looks to be a narcotic of sorts."

Taf leaned down and carefully searched the dead. He found a letter tucked within a coat pocket. It was far too easy to find.

One of the Royal Guard approached and stood at attention. "The King is secure. The castle is being evacuated now. We have had no other instances of violence."

"Any decent assassin will disappear with the crowd," Taf said. He rose and looked to Arma. "Check on the King."

Arma sheathed his sword and headed off.

"Dismissed," Taf told the Royal Guard.

He studied the dead face of the traitorous noble. How could a man who had been given so much in life be so selfish? Lord Dutha even had a father to raise and guide him. Some men were not even given that opportunity.

Taf flipped over the letter and pried it open with blood-stained fingers. He read over the simple instructions. The evidence damned Lathu as the mastermind to the plot. An assassination attempt ordered by one of Nestali's Ministers of Defense. Maybe war was on the horizon.

It made no sense. Taf slid the letter in his tunic, cleaned his blade, and hid it once more in his sleeve. At the very least, the King was safe.

BRUISING BATTLE
BURNING BRIARS

BRAERON'S HEART POUNDED in his ears louder than the slap of his hurried steps on the cold stones of the darkened hallway. Half-naked, bleeding, and covered in stars-knows-what, but he felt worse than he looked. *I've got to get out.*

He raced around the corner and stopped, bracing against the wall. The warm blaze of lanterns warmed the corridors in front of him. The light was too close for comfort. Braeron twisted about and slunk back the way he came.

The heavy darkness of Nathalem's underbelly left him scrambling with hands and feet. *I just had to take the job*, he grumbled to himself.

Easy money is never easy. His father's words felt more like a condemnation than a word to the wise.

Be nice if there was easy gold. He grabbed at his side as an old bruise reminded him of his earlier mistakes. Mercenary work wasn't exactly his preferred occupation, but the gold was good. Even if his parents were too stubborn to admit it, the family needed what he sent. Little Jak had himself a new pair of shoes last time Braeron visited. He couldn't help but smile when he thought about that. His brother had been so proud.

Light illuminated the end of the corridor in front of him. Cobwebs dangling from the ceiling reflected the glow in a gossamer sheen. The slick wet stones carried the voices of his previous jailers but jumbled the words beyond recognition. Behind and before, they were closing in on him. He wouldn't go back, not to a cage. He'd fight if he had to.

Braeron felt along the darkened wall until he stumbled upon a handhold. His fingers wrapped around the edge and he heaved himself upward, slapping the wall for more purchase. He twisted, kicked, and climbed until he managed to get hold of the ancient support beam running along the ceiling. The wood sagged as he struggled to pull himself into the rafters. A loud snap echoed in the damp stillness. Braeron felt himself falling.

He flipped himself over and jammed his legs into the darkness, somehow managing to find a hold on the rafters. Straining with back and core, he flexed himself into an awkward position with his arms and legs outstretched to divide the weight. Thankfully, the wood held, for now.

The light hurried closer. Voices started to take on actual words and curses.

The two gang members of the Crimson Briar approached. Braeron eyed the weapons hung about their belts. Fighting would be a self-imposed death sentence. The taller one hoisted a lantern that cast a glare across the corridor. Braeron could see his own arms shaking violently. *Don't look up.*

"Boss will be mad if we let this one get away," grumbled

the first.

"Probably find him a few weeks from now, once the stench gets bad."

Braeron felt his midsection starting to curl in on itself. He gasped as quietly as he could manage, sucking in air and feeling his chest tighten. He craned his neck and stifled a groan as his body started to cramp in twists and knots.

The next set of Briars joined the party. "Seen him?"

He gritted his teeth and breathed through the pain while he shifted his grip on the beam. Braeron felt a drop of sweat slither down his brow until it tickled his nose. It slipped off and shot down to the floor, missing the first guard. The next drop hit the closest Briar in the face.

"Stars," Braeron grumbled.

He swung down. The wood groaned then snapped in a shower of rotted, splintered chunks. He crashed into the ground. A shower of stones and splinters rained down. The torch light sputtered out, shrouding them in darkness. A low, menacing groan echoed across the walls.

Braeron rolled himself through the tangle of wooden debris, over a stunned Briar, until he felt solid stone. He stumbled into a limping jog down the corridor the way he'd come from. The grinding sound of shifting stone grew louder and louder until it rumbled into a thundering of crashing wood.

He walked, jogged, and limped into the darkness.

He stopped at the edge of the hallway, feeling empty air and knowing he needed to choose which direction to go. He'd memorized the route by imagining a sword drill and putting himself through the motion of attacking right or left. Now, he just needed to reverse it. He started from the end and went through the drill until he felt confident, not really, that he could get himself back.

He went right and headed down the hall until the next turn. He took a right and then a left. Left and right before another left. He repeated the drill over and over as he groped through the darkness with outstretched hands.

He turned a corner. The glow of torch light was visible at the end of the long hallway. Braeron almost shouted in triumph, clapping a hand over his own mouth. He knew where he was.

He hurried to reach one of the access tunnels. The crawlway was probably used by crews before the belly of Nathalem became occupied by gangs. He ducked under the low roof, crawled through, and carefully ascended the dilapidated ladder. Each rung produced a new groan or creak, but it held.

Easy gold. To the depths with it all. Most mercenary jobs included long weeks, lots of labor, and pay that hardly made it worth the trouble. Not to mention dealing with bandits or general rabble. From the moment they told him the sum, he should've turned and walked away.

These weren't a collection of fools, though. They lured him in with basic work that turned into questionable work that he could stomach for the gold. Finally he found himself in the midst of a kidnapping. That's where his morals got him in trouble.

He lifted himself onto the ledge barely big enough for two men. From where he stood he could see the entire cavern. Ancient architecture and aged infrastructure were all that was left of what must have been part of the original Nathalem. Whatever the purpose of the cavern used to be, it was now serving as the Crimson Briar's headquarters. It looked like someone had gutted a tavern and barracks, taken what was left and shoved it in between crumbling stonework.

To the right was a massive body of water black as night and only visible due to the reflection of light coming from the ruins. Stones that reminded him of bloated needles lay along the sides of the cave. The water was what drew most of his attention. He didn't want to think about what might live in the depths of the underbelly of Nathalem.

Braeron turned and frantically searched for the ladder that would lead up to the next level where he would continue his search for the surface. Only there was nothing on the walls. In the dim light he could see a crawlway going up, but how he would climb was undetermined. He knew at least one of them was still in use. The Briars boasted about using it. He'd just need to check them all.

Angry voices raged from below him. He glanced down to see the light pouring into the access tunnel. No reason to check in here. All he had to do was wait them out.

The light grew brighter. One of the gang members emerged into the access tunnel. Braeron pressed himself up against the wall.

"He's up here," called the man down below. "Whole lot of blood."

Braeron glanced over the edge. It was a long drop to the water. The ladder groaned. Maybe it would break. Braeron watched as two other members squeezed into the small space, torches blazing.

A flashback of the last time he almost drowned assaulted him. He pressed himself against the wall. He moved his toes just to be sure he was on solid ground.

The Briar reached the top of the ladder. He pulled out a sword. "Mutt," said the Briar. "Boss didn't say we needed to bring you back alive."

Braeron moved as far away as he could, which was not far enough. He eyed the sword. Dull or not, a length of metal could still do damage. The Briar stabbed from the ladder. Braeron avoided the awkward attack easily. The Briar swung in a wide arc. Braeron stepped back and fell onto one knee with his free leg dangling off the edge. He strained to get back onto the ledge.

"Got you now," the Briar said, stepping off the ladder. There was barely enough room for both of them to stand on the ledge.

The Briar stabbed in the same moment Braeron managed to get to his feet. He avoided the attack and grabbed the Briar's sword hand. Braeron fought to keep the steel from getting too close while the Briar pushed.

Braeron felt the exhaustion of poor food, little water, and the strain of his escape starting to take its toll. Eventually, the Briar would win.

Braeron looked the man in the eyes. "Can you swim?"

The Briar frowned. Braeron pulled backwards. They slipped off the edge. He wrapped his arms around the Briar's chest.

His stomach rose until it felt like it was stuck inside his ribcage. He tried to turn—

Darkness, a sharp, invasive chill, and the feeling of everything pressing in from all sides overwhelmed him. Braeron thrashed about, kicking away from the Briar. He felt his chest start to tighten. His feet found nothing below, and his arms seemed to carry him nowhere.

He felt the surface and surged out of the murky depths. Braeron gulped until he couldn't anymore. He clambered onto the shore, soaking wet. He flipped himself onto his back, giddy to be alive.

He remembered his unwilling travel companion. He crawled to the edge and listened for movement or breathing. The silence lingered long enough for him to wrestle with a twist of emotions. *Killed a man. He would've killed me.* Resolve settled the unease but could not dispel the feeling completely.

Now what? The question he'd been asking himself since the start of the day. Get out of the cage. *Great, but what happens next?* He heard voices from above and could see the light far above him. Would they be able to see him? Braeron watched orange glow cascading down.

He kept close to the wall, clambering around the strange rock formations until he reached the patchwork mess the Briars used as headquarters. He hunkered behind a good-sized rock and spent his efforts breathing and ignoring the pain in his limbs.

On the far end of the compound, past the majority of the Briars' operations, was a lift that led up to Nathalem proper. If he could get up to the surface, he could surprise the few guards and make a run for it. It was his worst option, but all the others were exhausted. *I guess I've exhausted myself.* He chuckled.

With a uniform, he might be able to move to the lift without drawing too much attention. *What I wouldn't do for a good pair of boots.* Some thug was probably defiling his last pair with their unkempt, smelly toes.

He waited until the watch settled and the compound grew quiet. He used the water to maneuver to where there were several cargo ships docked. He could slip into one of the barrels and wait it out. They had to move their cargo to the surface eventually.

He moved onto the docks, wary of patrols, and headed to the closest ship. Braeron peeked over the edge of the barge, checked to make sure no Briars were loitering about, then lifted himself onto the deck.

He checked again to make sure no one was patrolling nearby before he pried open the cargo hold. The dank, cramped corners of the lower deck were lit by the small rectangular windows lining the wall just by the ceiling. Braeron ducked his head and headed down.

For the first time all day, he tasted the possibility of freedom. *Learned my lesson,* he told himself.

His eyes started to adjust to the dim lighting at the same time his ears told him something was amiss. Coughs and the muttering of hushed voices made him take a step back up the stairs. There were no carts or boxes, only cages.

The prisoners were young, scared, and ragged. Camoor. The flat top of the first boy's ears gave them away. What in the depths were the Briars doing? Slavery wasn't exactly a profitable trade seeing as both Kingdoms condemned it as illegal. Maybe labor?

I need a new barge. Braeron headed back up the stairs and quietly lowered the hatch back on the cargo hold. What if all the barges had prisoners? *I've no mind to share the fate of these captives.*

Braeron froze. He couldn't leave them. These weren't just animals locked in a cage. These were people same as he.

He scanned the horizon before heading toward the captain's cabin on the ship. He tested the door and found it locked. Of course, it was locked. *I should leave.* It was the easier option.

At thirteen years of age, he'd left home for the army. Not because he wanted to, but because it felt right. He convinced them to take him into service and spent five long years marching and drilling and doing chores. Despite his time in the army, he still felt like the boy trapped back at home trying to figure out who he was and what he wanted to be when he got old enough. He still didn't know, and maybe he wouldn't ever, but he wasn't a coward, and he wouldn't let these people rot in a cage while he could do something about it.

Braeron fumbled about the ship for something heavy and found a discarded hammer. He tore off his mangled shirt and bit onto the cloth-wrapped handle of the tool while he climbed across the side of the ship. He reached the window looking into the captain's cabin.

He spread his shirt over the window and held it in place with his toes while wielding the hammer. He smashed the glass. It wasn't nearly as muffled as he wanted. He leaned out to see if any torches were swarming toward him and found nothing troublesome. Not yet, anyway.

He picked away at the glass, using the cloth before easing himself into the cabin through the recent remodeling. He started rummaging through the captain's desk. Letters, spilled ink, and a random assortment of knick-knacks filled the drawers. He felt the dark corners of the cluttered mess and found three keys, none of them similar. He took all of them.

Praise the stars. Braeron found some dried rations and, more importantly, a barrel of what he hoped was ale. He tore into the salted meat, washing it down with the tasteless, lukewarm piss they called ale.

A mess in the corner of the room caught his eye. He headed over, still drinking, and rummaged through the pile of dirty clothing. There was no uniform to be found, but it was a day of disappointments already. Despite the smell, he put on a shirt without holes and shoved a pair of boots under his arm. The leather was supple.

Braeron unlocked the cabin and hurried to the cargo hold. There were at least thirty souls caged like beasts. He set the boots aside and started to test the keys. His hands trembled from the work, his mind racing over the question he didn't want to ask. *How do I get them out?* Getting himself to freedom hadn't exactly worked. The first or second time.

Braeron unlocked the doors, one by one, until the captives were at least free of their immediate cages.

He walked over to the pair of boots he had recently liberated. A few of the captives braved stepping out of the cage, but none of them rushed for the deck. Mostly they watched him. Braeron took a pinch of salt from the sack he stole from the captain and sprinkled it inside of both boots before he slid his feet in to test the fit. Good leather. Malleable but resistant. They were too big.

Braeron tied the boots tight. Time for his third and most brilliant plan.

He looked to the gathering of boys and girls, realizing exactly who they were. The population of unattended youth that grew up in the shadow of Nathalem's High Town. Take what might not be missed. Some Katal got a sick pleasure from calling the young Camoor sewer rats.

"I'm going to need help."

A young girl, maybe ten years of age, stepped forward. "I'll do what I can. Don't want to fight."

"No fighting," said Braeron.

The work was long and slow, seeing as they needed to avoid being spotted by patrols and had to use the water to get to and from the ships. The rest of the cargo holds were filled with the usual illegal cargo. Fortunately, they found pitch and oil in good supply.

Braeron got everyone else in place before he sat on the edge of the ship where he'd found the prisoners. He drank from a stein of piss-poor ale. He was thirsty enough to be thankful. A passing pair of patrolling Brairs slowed to a stop, admiring him and his oversized boots.

"Evening," Braeron shouted.

The two men faced him, one of them toting a crossbow.

"Hope you don't mind. I'm taking this ship."

Braeron rolled onto the deck out of the way of the crossbow bolt. He scrambled over to the bell and started to ring it furiously. With the chime still reverberating in his ear, Braeron smashed a lantern on the pile of wood slathered in pitch. The flames roared to life. Braeron threw his makeshift raft over the side and jumped in after it.

He held onto the wood and paddled back toward the docks. Every one of the ships was on fire, spewing black into the cavern. No one noticed him slipping under the docks. Braeron used the network of wood under the pier to move through the water. Soon enough he caught up with the captives all afloat on their rafts moving toward the northern section of the docks.

Above them was a stampede of hurried feet, barked orders, coughs and curses. Smoke was starting to settle among the lower parts of the hideout. The thick, black clouds grew until it was almost impossible to see anything above them.

The escapees moved through the water until they reached the far end of the cavern. Braeron helped each of the captives get through the recently made hole in the floor before joining them in a crawl toward the lifting platform under the blanket of smoke.

"Faster now," Braeron said, urging the nearest captive. He looked behind him. Too many were lagging behind. How was he supposed to help if they didn't hurry?

He got up onto his knees and earned himself a face full of smoke. Coughing and cursing, he grabbed the nearest shoulder and yanked the boy forward.

"Move!" he sputtered.

The smoke lifted enough for him to see the feet of several Briars coming their way. *We've not enough time.* Braeron crawled toward the young girl furthest behind.

He got on one knee, wrapped his arm around her, and struggled to his feet. His eyes burned and his lungs wheezed, but he found his feet and ran.

"We need to go!" Braeron grabbed the shoulder of a straggler and practically dragged him toward the platform.

He coughed once, twice, and again. He dropped to a knee and struggled to stop the hacking. He felt all the weariness from the terrible day settling into his joints.

Braeron weakly urged the boy toward the platform. Braeron

crawled a few feet before crumpling to the ground. His chest tightened in another spasm of coughs. They should be safe. There were too many for the few Briars up top to stop. *I hope they all make it.*

He heard the pounding of feet as his captors drew closer. Braeron tried to rise but couldn't suppress his hacking.

Hands grabbed him and yanked him off the floor. They wouldn't let him rot away this time. A swift execution was sure to be in order.

Braeron felt the floor suddenly yank upward. He watched the platform lift away from the hideout and out of the clearing smoke. Several captives knelt nearby, holding onto him.

He could see several Briars looking up at them. Braeron mocked them with a dainty wave.

"Thanks for the lift," he shouted, and immediately started to cough.

ADMISSIONS AND ALCHEMY

I DO NOT HAVE ENOUGH. Kalliom moved the wooden pieces across the counting table for the fifth time in a row. Fifty thousand gold crowns. If he could secure the grant it would not be a problem, but the stingy group of wizened scholars were not known for their generosity.

He studied the extensive list. The problem was that he needed specialized equipment to ensure that his experiments were not a massive waste of time and gold. The tables needed to be metal, but the base would be a complex mechanism to ensure he could properly study the patients. What was the use of testing if he could not do his work thoroughly? Then there was the list of ingredients both rudimentary and exotic.

"Stars," he cursed. He leaned back in his chair and tapped the table while his mind stewed over the list of supplies he needed. He held his sun chart up to the window. Thankfully, his window faced west and he could check without moving. The falling sun was just between noon and early afternoon. Not much time before his scheduled meeting with the Board of Masters.

"I should get ready," he told himself.

"Do you always talk to yourself?"

Kalliom jumped out of his chair and whirled around. The speaker stood in the darkness of the eastern corner of his study. She, his unnamed advisor, had a habit of intruding unexpectedly.

"It helps direct neural activity and provide motivation," said Kalliom.

"If that helps you, I will keep my judgment but spare you the worst of it."

"The Crimson Briars failed to deliver. I spent a good portion of my own gold—"

She hushed him. "You are always so worried about gold."

Kalliom breathed out to calm himself. Who was she to belittle him so? "You may not suffer the restraint—"

"Even Kings are held captive to gold," she interrupted. "Those who find themselves with more than most can never have enough."

"I do not have enough. I will begin with my experiments as soon as we can procure subjects, but progress is bound to be slow."

She took a step forward. Kalliom grew rigid. Was it the thought of seeing who she was, or actual concern for his well-being? Both, he realized. She stepped out of the shadows, hood covering most of her face. He could see her lips colored a soft purple. She held out a stack of paper.

"I made some revisions to your presentation for the board."

"The audacity. As if you know better what the Masters want to hear."

"Your structure and argument lack nothing. You suffer not a deficiency of intelligence."

Kalliom reached out and took the pages. He swallowed the annoyance of his flattened ego before he skimmed the edits. There was almost nothing different with the first page.

He looked up. She was gone.

"I simply made a few adjustments. Word choices mostly. Thow are always so precise." She was sitting by the window with her legs crossed. The sun fell over her, giving her a golden glow that masked her features. "You lack imagination."

She rose, crossed the room and opened the door.

"Kalliom," she said, her words a hush. "I would prefer you do not fail me in this regard. The consequences would be...unpleasant."

Kalliom waited until she left the study, her bracelets clinking with every step, before he read the revised presentation. All she had done was change a few words. What he needed was gold, not correction on vernacular. He set down the corrections, picked up his own presentation, and slid it into his satchel.

Dressing for the occasion would be important. He chose a robe that was longer than he liked, colored green and white after his specialization. He carefully selected a collar that represented his most recent award as a member of the Leaders of Progress.

He checked himself in a polished stone. His hair was thinning, but he did what he could to make it seem less transparent. Haili said she didn't mind the age gap. No need to draw attention to it one way or another.

Smiling to himself, he gathered his things and thoughts. He could not remember the last time he found himself enamored by a woman. Not that he was considering a long term engagement.

Kalliom threw his satchel over his shoulder and opened the

door. Then he went back to his desk and swapped out his pages for the edited version.

The Library of Telem buzzed with students and teachers roaming the halls in between classes. It had been years since he had overseen a classroom. Not once did he miss the work. Research provided him greater opportunity to make actual progress.

He headed toward the council under the protection of covered walkways. Most of the library was stone and brick work. Windows stretching from floor to ceiling covered the outer wall of the first floor. Sunshine bathed the smooth white marble.

"Good afternoon, Master," said a passing student.

Kalliom acknowledged the young man with a nod of his head and nothing more. Many of the students he saw were first or second years. Still untested. If he were to guess, most of them would settle for a single ring and head off into the world as advisors or teachers for rabble of Ta'Thaloon.

He headed away from the sun-baked halls and into the musty, cramped tunnels of the administration wing. Several doors were open with clerks and assistants busy about their labors. He turned right, away from the archives, and traveled until he reached the far end of the library. The window at the end of the hall revealed the seemingly endless waters surrounding the island.

"Master," said the secretary to the Council of Twelve. The young woman was a sixth year with good marks who pandered to her superiors and had yet to earn a mastery.

"I will see myself in," Kalliom told her.

He walked past the woman and pushed open the large double doors. The room itself consisted of mostly wooden furnishings. It was organized with twelve chairs in a semicircle facing a table and a humble seat. Three massive windows on the far wall let in enough light to make the space feel distastefully bright.

Kalliom strode into the room with purpose. He produced his work, well mostly his, from his satchel and spread it out over the table. He moved the chair out of the way so he could stand as he delivered.

"Master Kalliom," called Master Lailim. She sat in the tallest of the chairs and served as head of processions.

"Master Lailim." Kalliom gave a polite bow.

None of the Board had changed hands since the passing of Master Omolli. That was a man who cared about progress. Several of the members had pushed Kalliom to take the vacancy, but he did not enjoy wasting his time on formalities. The Board oversaw everything from entrance applicants to Mastery examinations. Granted, if he did join one day he would never have to lecture again. Life was filled with hard choices.

Kalliom put his hands behind his back and waited for the procession to begin.

"Master Ghalli, do you accept the responsibility of overseeing the following processions?"

Kalliom watched the old man who was supposed to be taking notes. After a few painful moments of silence, the Master nearest the clerk shook his shoulder.

"Yes," Master Ghalli stated.

I do not recall him being so old. The thought made Kalliom painfully aware of his own age.

"Let us begin with our proceedings. The council recognizes that Master Kalliom has come before us to present a plea for a grant from the Library of Telem."

Kalliom tapped his right foot impatiently. All of this was a waste of time. *Give me the gold so I can get on with it.*

"Typically, this is overseen by a committee. However, due to the size of the grant requested, the Board has unanimously decided to oversee the procession in assembly."

Kalliom's foot stopped flat on the floor. *Unanimously?*

"Before we begin the formalities of the debate, I think it is worth saying that we all recognize your contributions to the Library and by no means wish to draw in question your time or efforts therein."

Not a good start.

"Would anyone else care to add anything before we begin?"

Kalliom clenched his hand. No one else said a word.

"Let us begin." Master Lailim spread a few sheets in front of her. "You are going to present your petition verbally. Is that correct?"

Master Ghalli started writing furiously.

"Yes," Kalliom replied.

"We will proceed by asking a question, after which you will give an account. The board will follow with a retort, and then you will finish with a defense."

It felt like one of his verbal exams. They always tried to throw him. Especially on his last and sixth ring. Probably due to jealousy; mastering Alchemy had given him one more ring than even Master Ballakim. Last he checked, the wizened Master was still struggling with course work on his next ring. Kalliom had more important projects now than rings and achievements. Progress was a better mistress anyway. Maybe not as good as Haili.

Master Lailim cleared her throat. "What is the project in

question, and what do you intend to accomplish within the parameters of your research?"

Kalliom checked the rough answer and noted the changed words.

"The project in question is targeted at understanding and utilizing the findings of the late Master Cai'Tallai in order to better understand and assist in neural instability."

Her word choices were softer and more appealing. It almost made it sound like his intent was one founded in altruism rather than conquest.

"This indicates that the realm of study falls more in line with medicine than your outline suggests," said one of the Masters.

The body withers. Medicine is a waste of time. "It certainly falls within the realm of body science."

"How do you intend to capitalize on what you understand of Master Cai'Tallai's work to ensure that time and effort are not wasted?" asked Master Lailim.

What she had written was only half the truth. Practically a lie. Thow did not lie. Kalliom steadied his pulse.

"I intend to secure participants for the study."

"And how will you acquire these individuals?" one of the Masters asked.

Any means necessary. "I have contacts that I will utilize to coerce those who are willing to suffer the possible side effects."

"Do the side effects in question pose a concern for the participants?" asked Master Lailim.

Master Ghalli held his pen above the page, but his gaze was on Kalliom, along with the entire council.

Kalliom swallowed his pride and took the response penned by his associate. "It is difficult to tell. What little I understand indicates that Master Cai'Tallai's work was intended to assist in stabilizing. It is the hope and goal of this study to comprehend and expound on the knowledge acquired, but the participants will be monitored closely to ensure that the process is successful."

"You stated earlier that the goal of this study is neural stability. The realm of the mind remains a great mystery. How do you intend to ensure that you do not cause permanent harm to the participants?" asked one of the Masters.

"The reason why I have appealed for a grant of this size is to provide myself with every opportunity to ensure the process is done carefully. Madness and emptiness of the mind have always perplexed even those of us who have some understanding of the intricacies of the brain. I will oversee every individual's process myself to ensure that no mishaps take away from the success of the study."

Master Ghalli's pen scribbled furiously. The scratching filled the absence of spoken words.

Master Lailim picked up her page and studied it.

What are they waiting for?

"Master Kalliom," started Master Lailim, setting down the page. "I must confess that I am still confused as to the end goal of the research. It appears to me that you simply intend to capitalize on the work of a brilliant man who never reached any conclusions. Are you not concerned that your efforts will be as fruitless as those before?"

"The reason that we study and test and consider is to overcome the past and guide Ta'Thaloon into the future." Kalliom twisted one of his rings back and forth. "I will admit that it is overwhelming to consider taking up the mantle of a Thow of unparalleled genius, but time continues its endless march, and I do not overlook my age. I have ever dedicated myself to learning. This to me seems an appropriate endeavor to carry me to the grave."

Many of the council members nodded their understanding. Master Ghalli kept writing, not missing a sentence, apparently.

Master Lailim set the pages down and looked down at Kalliom. "I find myself intrigued as to the knowledge you will be capable of finding. I do wish for clarity. I am still no nearer to understanding what you intend to accomplish."

Domination of the mind. Control. Subjugation. "It is my goal to address the issue of neural instability and provide insight into how to best care for the individuals who suffer from it."

"Your goal is ultimately to provide healing?" asked one of the Masters.

"I believe the research will help remedy some of the suffering Ta'Thaloon experiences."

"You are not certain?" asked Master Lailim.

"Certainty is won over time and testing."

Master Lailim adjusted her pages. "I have no further questions. Would anyone else care to address the subject at hand?"

Kalliom waited. The room grew uncomfortably silent. What a waste of time.

"Very well," said Master Lailim. "Let us bring the matter to a vote. Let every member of the council who wishes to supply Master Kalliom with the requested grant please raise their hands."

Two hands went up immediately. Another followed. A third. Kalliom masked his disappointment and gritted his teeth. The fools. Who were they to stand in way of progress?

Master Ghalli raised his hand and Master Lailim soon after. Four others joined them soon after.

"The vote is cast. Nine in favor and three opposed." Master Lailim put the papers to the side. "Master Kalliom, I look forward to studying your progress. Does the council have any more business?"

Kalliom twisted one of his rings back and forth. He would dip into his own funds and start recruiting while he awaited the paperwork to finalize. The Crimson Briars, who would be the most obvious choice, were apparently incapable. He would use them, if only because his advisor insisted.

A better and faster source was available. There were a few ship captains who took on Camoor rabble at a low labor cost. They might be willing to assist in procuring recruits, especially since gold was no longer an issue.

"Without further questions, we can move to adjourn this meeting. The Board thanks you for your time, Master Kalliom."

Master Kalliom dipped his head respectfully. "I thank the council for their time and support. May it be that together we work toward shaping the future of Ta'Thaloon."

THE BEST
MEDICINE

JATHALOR PRESSED HIS EAR against the door
and listened. Another bout of shallow, harsh coughs wheezed
from inside the room. He needed to do something to help Pa.

The handle to the door rumbled before it swung open. The
healer, who happened to be the cook as well, motioned Jathalor
away from the door.

"Get on," grumbled the man. "No sense giving the cold away."

Jathalor caught a glimpse of his Pa lying in bed with a towel
over his head just before the door slammed shut.

"Pa's going to be better, right?" asked Jathalor.

The healer grumbled something else as he shuffled toward
the stairs leading up to the deck. He was a tall, crooked man with
large hands and beady eyes. None of his food was any good.

Jathalor turned back to the door and pressed his ear
against the scratchy wood. One of the men said lots of people
died to a cold. Said it was bad on the sea because of the damp
and cold. He listened, heart thumping in his chest, as his Pa
hacked and wheezed.

He had to do something. He rushed to the crew quarters, dodging other sailors while hurrying onto the deck. He ducked behind some of the crates being off-loaded to avoid the gaze of the captain. The tall, strong Katal was good with the helm and always seemed to know what to do, but Jathalor couldn't help feeling a bit uncomfortable around him.

He took the steps to the crew quarters two at a time. He pried open the chest he and Pa shared, rummaging around at the bottom until he found the silver coin shoved into the corner. He was going to find medicine and nothing would stop him.

With the silver coin, the only one he brought on this voyage, safely in his pocket and a mind full of ideas where to look, what could possibly go wrong?

Jathalor bounced down the catwalk.

"Be back before nightfall," called a loud, commanding voice.

Jathalor stopped, turning around to see the captain at the edge of the deck looking right at him. He forced himself to smile. "I'll be back," he told the captain.

Jathalor hurried down the catwalk with a newfound urgency, leaving the pier and the ship he worked on behind him. Several other men were moseying their way into the city. He didn't know what adults did with their time once the work was done, and he didn't spend too much time thinking about it. His mind needed to be on finding a healer.

The city was different. Lots of buildings, not nearly as tall as those in Nathalem. He could see the ocean stretching to the west. The port moved like a fish's belly, curving around until it connected with the Founder's River. It had taken them three days of sailing to get here. How big was the world?

He left the port and found himself surrounded by buildings on all sides. There were shops with all sorts of strange pictures. People were headed this way and that. It was a lot of strangers, but not as many as were in Nathalem at night, at least he didn't think so.

Jathalor stopped and looked north and south. There were so many streets and places to go. He looked to the sky and remembered the captain's warning. He hurried down the nearest street and started to look for an adult who might know things about healing and, what was the other word? *Tinures? No. Pa said it was like the tinkling of glass. Tinctures.*

He walked straight and didn't wander right or left. It would be easier getting back to the ship if all he needed to do was turn around.

He walked beneath the shadow of buildings of different shapes and sizes. Some with painted signs and others with words he could not read engraved onto imposing wooden doors. One of the pictures looked to be a pot of some kind with steam roiling out of it. This seemed like a good place to ask about tinctures. He tested the door and found it closed, so he continued his search.

Alleys occasionally broke up the congested buildings. Even in the waning light it was hard to see more than a few feet into the shrouded stretch. Jathalor hurried past every alley.

"I don't see what you're doing!" The voice was distorted and ragged.

Jathalor looked for the speaker but saw no one around him. There were a few people a ways off but they could not sound so close, could they?

"What you're doing!"

Jathalor shifted his gaze downward and found a man sitting just outside an alley, one leg outstretched. He had a collection of trash about him. His face was dirty and several of his teeth were missing. Plenty of his sort in Nathalem. Sometimes Pa called them mean names.

"I don't know what you mean," said Jathalor. He wondered why the man let himself smell of bad cheese. Did his nose not work?

"I don't see what you're doing. Out past the light. Wandering about."

"I just need medicine. It's for my Pa. He's not feeling well and I've got to get something for his head."

The smelly man shuffled back and forth, drawing his leg into the mess of crumpled paper and splintered wood like a spider pulling back into its refuge. "Best thing for the head is to drink and drink and drink."

Jathalor watched the man start to rise. *Don't let a stranger get too close.* The man found his feet. *Run!* He tried to move. He couldn't even wiggle his toes.

"What your Pa need? Is it hot or cold he feel?"

Jathalor found his courage and started to run.

"Be going wrong," the man called after him. "Back ways."

Jathalor didn't stop. He ran until he couldn't anymore, and then he checked to make sure the smelly man wasn't close. Pa'd be mad that he let himself get so close to a stranger who wasn't working. He pressed up against a wall and breathed until the stitch in his side didn't grab at him every time he moved.

"You there," called out a Law Keeper. There were two men walking side by side toward him. They both had swords at their sides and crisp brown uniforms with purple and gold sashes across their chests. Their tricorn hats held their pins of service on the front right sides.

He could hear his Pa talking him through how to handle being addressed by a Keeper. Head down, voice even and answers quick and not annoying.

Jathalor lowered his head and waited until the men were right up on him.

"What are you stalking about for? Especially at this hour." Jathalor didn't need to look up to feel the weight of the two men staring down at him.

"I wasn't stalking."

"What are you doing?"

Jathalor swallowed the knot in his throat. "Looking for medicine. For my Pa, he's got a head cold."

The Keeper laughed. "Did your Pa tell you what to get? Let me guess, something brown that burns as it goes down."

"None of them spirits, sir." Jathalor swallowed his long explanation. These men didn't care. Especially not about him, a Camoor.

The Keeper regarded him with critical eyes. "Keep out of trouble. I do not want to find you drinking any 'medicine.'"

The men moved around him and Jathalor waited until they were a few feet down the road to lift his head. He wanted to run after them and beg for help. Maybe they'd listen if he told them his Pa was in bed. He never found the courage.

Jathalor walked down the street, his feet dragging. The sunlight was nearly spent and he'd nothing to show for it.

He studied the buildings as he went. Through the windows, he could see objects tall and slender, fat and pretty. The treasures were unlike anything he'd seen before. On the other side of the street, where the shadows were long, the windows were shrouded. Inside, the shapes were twisted and bent. He thought he saw something move. He hurried down the street.

The places that might sell medicine, at least the signs that were most promising, were all locked. He knew he was running out of time and decided to ask the next adult he met. Someone would know something about someone who knew medicine. Adults knew about such things.

He found a few adults hanging outside a building that wasn't locked. It was down a side road, but he knew he could find his way back to this street. He nearly ran up to the first person.

"Miss," he started, struggling to find enough time to breathe between words. "I'm looking for medicine. I know it's late now and not many are up, but I need something for my Pa. He's got a head cold."

The woman didn't even look down at him. She was wearing clothing without enough cloth to cover all of her. It didn't seem good for keeping warm.

"Miss?"

Another woman walked over and knelt down. He could see several bruises on her arms. "You've no business being about this late at night. Where are your parents?"

"Pa's sick is all. I need something for a head cold."

The other woman glanced down at him. "No sense being about. There's nothing to be found this late."

Jathalor looked at the woman who actually seemed to care. "Have you any idea?"

"What is going on?" asked a grumpy-looking man in a long coat.

The woman rose quickly. She looked to be about to speak when the grumpy man grabbed her arm.

"Is this a potential customer?" asked the man.

"Stars, no."

"Then leave him be."

Jathalor watched the woman walk away. She gave him a quick glance that told him all he needed to know about her sympathy. If she could, she would help him.

"Get on," said the grumpy man. He made a shooing motion at Jathalor. "Get off my street."

Jathalor knew better than to argue with an adult, especially an adult with a pinched face and wild eyes.

He hurried back the way he came and stopped at the end of the street. This was the path that he took from the ports, wasn't it? He looked this way and that trying to find something, anything that might remind him that this was where he came from. The light was almost spent. He had to try to help Pa.

Determined, he headed farther into the city. The smell of the salt water was gone from the air and the buildings started to look lonelier.

Jathalor turned to the side. He heard something. He looked behind and in front of him. Checking to the right and then the left, he found nothing apart from the lonely street. The sound was closer this time. It was a sharp, high-pitched animal noise. He had heard something like it back in Nathalem when he ran into a wild dog.

The sound came from behind him. Jathalor turned around and looked down at a small, furry dog. The animal wagged its tail back and forth menacingly. The dog barked at him, tilting its head to the side, and giving him an inquisitive expression.

He remembered, suddenly and vividly, the last time he'd seen one of these animals. It chased him down a street. He felt the teeth sinking into his leg.

Jathalor took a step back. "Stay," he told the dog.

The small animal jumped to its feet and barked. Jathalor turned and ran. He checked behind him to see if the dog was following. It stayed seated with its tail flailing back and forth behind it.

Jathalor sighed. Good thing it wasn't hungry. He turned and continued his search.

A few steps down the street Jathalor stopped. He thought he heard the sound of something behind him. He turned around to see the small animal sitting and looking right at him. It didn't seem any farther away.

Jathalor walked and then turned around suddenly. The small animal was on its feet, as if it were going to follow. Its eyes were wide and its mouth open, tongue hanging out.

Fear drove Jathalor to run as fast as he could, ignoring the shadows of the alleys and the empty stores with their unknowable depths. The light was gone, the colors of sunset staining the sky. He found a building with light and pushed on the door, praying to whatever gods the Katal worshiped.

The door swung open. Jathalor collapsed inside and breathed until he felt his heart steady.

The room stank of cramped bodies and sweat. Several gruff-looking men and women were watching him. Jathalor stood as soon as he had the strength. He headed to the nearest table. He'd already wasted too much time. Pa would not be happy that he was out so late.

"Pardon," Jathalor said. "I need—"

"Get on," one of the women told him.

Jathalor walked to the next table. "Pardon." The closest man pushed him away.

He could hear them snickering while they watched him. He didn't understand their side glances or why they cared to follow him at all. He just needed someone to tell him where to find medicine.

"What, boy?" growled a man with a quivering jowl. His hair was missing on the top of his head but thick on the sides. "You aren't serving drinks, so piss off."

"I need medicine, for my Pa. He isn't feeling right. Got him a head cold."

The man eyed him. Jathalor didn't like him. Not just because he smelled bad or had beady eyes. Something about him seemed wrong.

"Need coin to buy medicine, isn't that right?"

"I've enough," Jathalor reassured the man. "Just need to know the way."

The man drank from his stein, set it on the table, and eased out of the stool. He was tall and rotund.

"I'll show you, come on then."

Jathalor followed the man, ignoring the expressions of all the unhelpful people in the room. Finally, he was going to find some medicine so he could help his Pa. He wanted to tell the man just how thankful he was for the help, but he didn't want to be bothered.

They stepped outside, the air feeling colder than it had before. Night had settled in leaving a sky full of shining stars and a great swirling mess of green. People called the collection of sky

The Garden. He was late, but he was going to get medicine. A few lashings were worth it.

The man walked them down the street and stopped.

"I thank you. Which way do I go?" Jathalor gave his best smile.

"How much you got in coin?" the man asked. He held his large, sweaty palm out.

Jathalor stepped back, hand on his pocket. "I've enough."

The man stepped toward him and grabbed Jathalor by the shoulder. He squeezed until it started to hurt. "Let's see."

Jathalor felt his face growing warm. No reason to cry; the pain wasn't so bad. Wasn't the feeling anyway. Why were people so mean? All he wanted was to help.

"Hold up!" shouted someone from behind.

"None of your business," the man said, looking past Jathalor.

The newcomer spoke, and he sounded stern and mean. "This doesn't look like any of yours."

"This is my coin," the man spat. "Go get your own sewer rat to steal from."

"I've enough drink to do something stupid," said the person behind Jathalor.

The large man stepped away from Jathalor and held his hands out. His face was twisted in fear. Jathalor didn't want to look to see. If this man was afraid, he should probably be scared too.

"I'd say you've enough for the night. Pay your tab and be about your sleep. Maybe think about what you would've done here."

"It's just a sewer rat. No harm here. I'll be using his coin better than he would anyway."

"I said get going."

The meaty man clenched his fists. "You've no right to give me a lesson. I know who you are. One of them worthless coinswords you are."

"I've a mind to show you why I'm paid." The newcomer stepped forward, sword in hand and brandished at the meaty man. "You've some coin on you, I bet?"

The meaty man gave the newcomer a large berth as he walked around and back toward the warm building.

"Leave some for the waitress." The newcomer slid his sword back into its scabbard.

Jathalor stood frozen in fear as the man turned to look at him. The stranger wasn't exceptionally tall, but he was strong about the chest and shoulders. He looked to be ordinary, dark hair and the patchy start of a beard on his face. His hands were veined and gnarled from work like most Camoor, but this was definitely a Katal.

"Braeron," the stranger said, holding out his hand in greeting. Jathalor hesitated.

"We don't need to shake," said Braeron. "Hope I didn't scare you or nothing. Just didn't want to see anything bad happen to you. Didn't think I'd talk him out of it, so I used what I had."

Jathalor felt all the confusion and frustration of the night boil inside of him. "Why would he be that way?"

Braeron looked the way his Pa did whenever he was thinking about what he was about to say. "I don't know. Been asking myself that a lot of late."

"Are you going to take my coin?"

"Stars, no." Braeron closed his mouth. "Pardon the language. My mother would flog me for saying as much before someone so young."

95

Jathalor always wondered what it was like to have a mother. He also worried this man was still going to take his coin. Everyone else seemed to want to take from him.

"What're you doing out so late? Not many Camoor live in the port proper. You work around the docks?"

"On a ship," Jathalor told him. His Pa would tell him not to talk to strangers.

"Best we get you back, then," said Braeron.

Jathalor didn't want to go alone, but he didn't need to be going with a stranger. He could run. There was something different about this man. The meaty man felt wrong, like he wasn't right, and Braeron felt the other way. But could he be trusted?

He let out a breath from frustration. Why was helping so hard?

Braeron pulled off his coat and handed it to Jathalor. "You look cold."

Jathalor stared at the coat. It was the good kind of leather, with a bit of fur lining the inside. Nicer than anything he'd ever worn.

Braeron yawned. "Shouldn't have had that last one. That's something else my mother might flog me for, so let's keep my drinking habits between you and me. Let's see. Coast is..."

Jathalor pointed back toward the coast. He knew it had to be back. He'd traveled one direction.

"That's right," Braeron said and started walking toward the coast.

Jathalor thought about dropping the coat and running. It was warm and soft to the touch.

"Come on," Braeron called.

Jathalor hesitated but hurried to catch up with Braeron, sliding the coat, that was far too big, on his arms. He watched Braeron with every step.

They walked side by side. The buildings seemed more like they were when the light still gave everything clarity.

"What's this about you making trouble this late at night?" asked Braeron.

"I didn't mean no trouble."

"No one so young has any business being about so late."

Jathalor looked down at his feet. His Pa would be mad.

"I just wanted to help," said Jathalor.

Braeron said nothing, but he had a look about him like he was somewhere far from where they walked. "That's what I tell myself. Every day."

"You know where medicine might be?" asked Jathalor, hopeful.

Braeron looked down at him with his brows all bunched together. "Can't say I do. Father told me Alchemy was from the depths. Took to healing most of my problems with the best medicine."

"What's the best medicine?" asked Jathalor.

"Good friends, sunshine, and sleep."

"My Pa has lots of sleep."

Braeron stopped them. "Do you see that there?"

Jathalor looked. It was the menacing dog from before.

Braeron knelt down and patted his legs, whistling. What was he doing? Did he want the animal to attack?

The dog bounded toward them. Jathalor took a step back and used Braeron as a shield. It was a cowardly act, but he didn't want to be bitten. Not again.

Braeron wrestled the dog to the ground. He pinned the ferocious beast and started to—rub its stomach.

"That's a good boy," said Braeron. "This here's a snake catcher.

97

Had one just like it back on the farm. Though this one's nothing but a pup."

Jathalor peeked from behind Braeron. Seeing the small animal on its back with its tongue sticking out made it seem less imposing.

"Go on then," said Braeron. "He won't bite."

"You sure?"

"Sure am. One of the best parts of a pup is they haven't had anyone teaching them nothing wrong. This is the way a dog supposed to be."

Jathalor dared to take a step around Braeron. "Been bitten once."

"Shame that is. Nothing you did. Probably had someone beat it."

Jathalor looked down at the happy pup. It was nudging Braeron's hand. "Why would anyone do that?"

Braeron patted the pup and stood up. "Wish I knew. I'd change it if I could."

Jathalor reached out. The dog opened its mouth. Jathalor closed his eyes, ready for pain. The feeling that came was not bad, but weird. He opened his eyes and watched the dog lick his hand before nudging his fingers with its wet nose.

He touched the dog's head. Its fur was soft, and its ears were floppy. Jathalor stroked the pup's back and it seemed to like it.

"He'll probably follow us now. Wish I had the means to care for him. Doubt the captain will let him on the ship."

Jathalor felt his stomach sink as he rose. Captain's orders were to be back before or right after nightfall. By the time they got back he was going to be late. *Why am I always in trouble?*

They kept walking side by side, the stars shining bright. The dog padded behind them. Jathalor liked the sound of its pattering.

"Bit of advice," said Braeron. "If you don't mind me saying so."

Jathalor shook his head.

"When you got coin, don't tell no one. People you trust maybe, but I've known friends become enemies over a few pieces."

Jathalor listened and wondered. Braeron wasn't that old. Not like some of the other people he knew, and yet he seemed to know so much.

"Trick I learned while serving is to shove some into your sock. No one wants to look there."

"I don't have socks," Jathalor said.

"Shove it in your boots then. Hold it between your toes when someone goes to check for it."

They passed the street where the women were standing outside in their sparse clothing. Braeron didn't even look in their direction.

Jathalor wondered what he could do for his Pa. He could be a friend, but he was already a son. Maybe he needed to be better. He could get his Pa out for sunshine, but he was always so tired.

The smell of salt in the air made Jathalor realize how close they were. The journey before seemed like an entire day. He saw a building that looked familiar and then saw the alley with the beggar. He put Braeron between him and the shadows.

"Is it hot or cold he feels?" The sound came from the smelly man.

"Leovli," said Braeron. "What are you doing this side of town?"

"Sleep where sleep is."

Jathalor looked up at Braeron. He didn't seem to mind the smell or the strange way the man talked.

"What's this about cold or hot?"

"Does he know hot or cold?" Leovli asked, looking right at Jathalor.

Jathalor didn't understand what the man wanted from him. He'd not done anything to him or tried to bother him.

"I think he's asking after your father," said Braeron. "You said you needed medicine."

"Pa has a head cold."

"Hot or cold?" Leovli asked.

Jathalor felt uncomfortable as the strange man stared at him intently.

"He's asking if your father feels hot or cold."

Jathalor had to think a bit about it. He had felt his Pa's forehead the day before. It was cold but his Pa said he felt hot.

"Pa told me he's hot. Felt cold to me," Jathalor said, doubting himself even as he said it.

Leovli vanished into the alley. The pup wandered into the shadows with its nose to the ground.

"Ah!" gasped Leovli from the darkness. He emerged from the shadows, walking away from the pup who was right on his heels.

"No harm there," said Braeron. "Just wants to smell you is all."

"No good smell here," Leovli said.

Braeron laughed. "That there pup thinks different."

Leovli held something out in front of Jathalor. He took it from the strange man, expecting it to feel dirty, but there was nothing wrong with the package. He unwrapped the supple leather to find packed leaves that smelled of spring.

"Should've thought about that," said Braeron. "Mother used to give us a tea smelled like that when we'd been out in the rain."

"Thought your father didn't like Alchemy," Jathalor said.

"Sure, but my mother didn't care what my father thought. She'd go around him all the time. Always told us he was just stubborn and not to mind him being himself." Braeron smiled down at the pup nudging Leovli's ankles. "Best you pet him, or her, never did check. Won't leave you alone otherwise."

"Best to leave."

"I have myself thinking the other way. I can't give that pup a home. Maybe it's best you two be getting along."

Leovli looked up at Braeron with a wildness about his eyes. "No good here."

Braeron stepped closer to Leovli. "You and I both know that's no truth. Think about this boy here. Took care of him, did you. It would be good for you two to have each other. I've a mind to say the stars were at work tonight."

The pup stared directly up at Leovli and whined. Jathalor found himself feeling uncomfortable with the stillness. Why didn't he just pet the dog? Maybe he'd been bitten before too. Pa said that people were hard because life wasn't often kind and living wasn't always easy.

Leovli finally leaned over and petted the dog awkwardly on the head. The pup nudged his hand. Jathalor watched as Leovli smiled, and to him it felt like something important had just happened even if he didn't know why.

"Let's get you back," said Braeron, putting a hand on Jathalor's shoulder.

They left the two alone and headed for the docks. Jathalor slipped the leather into his pocket and felt the coin waiting there.

"I forgot," Jathalor said. He hurried over to Leovli and held the coin out. The man took it, a confused expression on his face. "Thank you much."

Jathalor hurried to catch up with Braeron. They left the shadows of quiet buildings and reached the docks.

Jathalor listened to the clomp of their feet on the boards of the docks. The memory of his leaving came with the terrible reminder that he was late to be reporting back and the captain would be mad.

"This is the ship," said Jathalor. He turned to face Braeron and found himself wishing he had something to give as a way of thanks. He didn't know what the night would've been without the help. "Thanks."

"Glad to help."

Jathalor stopped just before the gangplank. He didn't want to face the captain, but he needed to give his Pa the medicine.

"I can walk you aboard," Braeron said. "Assuming the captain don't take offense to me coming on."

"He's only going to take offense at me being late." As if speaking the words brought the wrath to life, the captain emerged on the gangplank.

"I'll vouch for what you've been doing."

Jathalor shook his head. "A few lashings is all. Thank you all the same. You know, you're different."

"I'll take that as a kindness."

"You should. I only mean it to say I wish more Katal were like you." Jathalor started the dreadful walk up the gangplank to face the red-faced captain waiting for him. He didn't even pretend to know words to explain himself. Take the punishment and see to his father. It was enough to bear the lash.

The captain tapped his foot. "Been out, have you?"

"Yessir."

"And what have you be doing about so late?"

"Disobeying."

The captain ushered him aboard. The first mate, a large brooding man with ink covering both his arms and neck, stepped up behind Jathalor.

"I'll take my lashing," said Jathalor. "I know I've done wrong."

"No lashing today," the captain said. "Take him to the brig. We'll drop him off before first light. Don't want anyone else even hearing about his coming back. Gone off into the dark he has."

No lashing. How could he be so lucky? Time in the brig was lonely but it didn't hurt.

"Give this to my pa?" Jathalor asked, holding out the leather-wrapped herbs. "I think he knows what to do with it."

The captain took the bundle and unwrapped it. He gave the contents a sniff. "Nothing to be done with a bunch of dry weeds. Can't even smoke this."

"Please, sir."

"To the brig with you. I'll get your father his dried flowers."

A ROSE IS FOR ROMANCE

TAF STOOD AT THE DOOR with his fist raised to knock. He lowered his hand. It had been years since he last went on a date. The distinct feeling of boredom mixed with embarrassment roiled in his gut. Lady Lavisli still refused to look him in the eyes.

Taf tried to push those thoughts out of his head, but the discomfort in his stomach refused to settle.

He struck his chest and cleared his throat. "Good evening," he practiced. "Nice to see you again. Evening. Nice night."

He sighed, feeling defeated. He had known Maisali for years. There was a time he thought they were going to be married, but now, after so long? She had agreed to the date, but it felt like an act of compassion. Maybe it would have been best to leave the past in the past and get over himself.

The nobles' housing compound was a sprawling complex of beautiful buildings and manicured gardens. The fading sun caught on the edge of the waxy leaves. A breeze blew overhead, ruffling the branches. Memories of past nights stirred somewhere deep within him. They used to walk often and long in these gardens, talking of life and dreams, hopes and failures.

Taf reached down to straighten one of the roses. He grabbed the stem.

"Stars," he grumbled, pulling his finger off the thorn.

"I know I look good," said his date. "But I did not think I looked that good."

Taf looked away from the blood oozing from his finger. Maisali was standing in the door, in a purple dress with a white shawl about her shoulders. She did not look good. There were no words to capture her. She was more beautiful than anything else in all of Ta'Thaloon.

Taf fumbled over several words before he managed a rough-sounding "greetings."

"It is good to see you too. Did you know you are bleeding?"

Taf sucked the blood off his finger before he pinched his thumb onto the wound. He handed her the roses.

She laughed at him. His heart fluttered uncomfortably. *I should not have asked.*

"You have not changed," Maisali said. She took the flowers from him. "These are lovely. Thank you." She kissed him on the cheek. "I should put them in water. Give me a moment."

The door shut in Taf's face. He felt his chest compress. He patted down his hair, then remembered he was bleeding and frantically wiped to make sure he did not have blood on his forehead. The door swung open.

Lady Masaili headed down the stairs and walked past him. "You have something," she said, looking back at him and motioning to his forehead. "Just there."

106

Taf fell in line beside her while trying to clean off the blood.

"I take it we are not doing anything out of the ordinary?" Maisali asked. "Let me see if I remember. A walk through the King's Gardens after a light supper on the terrace?"

"We can do something else, if you would prefer."

"I did not say I wanted to do anything else."

Taf glanced over. Her hair caught the fading sun like a halo of gold. She had always been younger, but now she looked ages from him. Especially with the wrinkles starting to crowd his eyes.

"Eastwatch is an interesting court," Maisali started. "You might prefer it actually."

"What would make you say that?"

"The nobles are more...common. If that is permissible to say."

Taf put his hands behind his back. It was his preferred way to walk. "How so?"

"The court itself resides within the castle rather than being housed in a separate compound, which I attribute as being a major factor. As you know, the city was almost an accident."

"I know the gist of the story. Northern pilgrims took refuge while the King held Eastwatch against invaders. The refugees stayed."

"I assumed the court would suffer from the politics of Nathalem, but it seems to me that the court shapes the noble."

Taf mulled the thought. "You have not changed."

"What do you mean?"

"You are still yourself. Intelligent, concerned." *Unmarried. Stunning. Younger than myself.*

"Taf, have you changed at all?"

Taf put his hand on the sword at his hip. It was the same one the King had gifted him before he and Maisali met. "I am old."

"Older," said Maisali. "I hope you are not completely void of vigor."

Taf felt his face getting red. "I can fight well enough."

High Town was starting to show signs of night life. Lanterns were being lit outside taverns and smoke shops. Young couples walked hand in hand, busy with the lack of concerns only youth provided. He never knew that life. With his father gone there was always work to be found and done.

Reality came crashing back in when he realized he was half a step ahead of his date. Poor manners. Taf struggled to find something to say, an apology, maybe. He settled for a question.

"Tell me, what have you found for yourself to do in Eastwatch? If I can remember, you were never one to stand by idle."

"Other than dating nobles?"

Taf swallowed the jumble of questions that came to mind. She mocked him with a knowing smile.

"Of course. It is assumed you have most of the court asking after you. How do you accomplish anything with so many suitors?"

"I have my ways," she said.

They ascended the stairs that led to the pavilion overlooking the King's Gardens. The matron overseeing the dining area did not have to ask for Taf's identification. He ate here often, if for nothing else than to relive the memory of younger days.

Taf could not help but notice the eyes following them as they went to sit at the table with the best view of the Gardens. He pulled back his chair and sat in a single motion.

"Apologies," he stammered, rising to get her chair.

"I can seat myself," insisted Maisali.

Taf sighed. "I am a bit of an embarrassment. Thank you, for your company and grace."

"You moved on," Maisali said.

Taf looked over at her. Her eyes were still piercing and perceptive, but there was no judgment in her gaze, just a touch of sorrow.

"The first month I followed our past like a ghost haunting the only memory it could remember. I think I may have even carried on conversation. I never moved on. I mourned."

Maisali did not have a reply. The lack of anything witty, more than the silence, left him bothered. This date was a bad idea. Dredging up skeletons from the past never proved worthwhile.

Regardless, he should and would behave like a proper date. "You never answered my question," Taf pointed out.

A young Camoor dressed in a white blouse set glasses of wine in front of them.

"Oh, you mean the boring question about what I do with my time."

That was the Maisali he knew. "Apart from dating nobles."

"Which is what I do with most of my time."

"What else do nobles do anyway?"

She took a sip of wine and he followed suit.

"Honestly," Maisali said. "It has been encouraging. As I mentioned, the court is not as structured, for lack of a better word, as the one here in Nathalem. Do you remember the labor policy we talked about?"

"How could I forget? They conceded to a policy related to the matter two weeks past."

"That is why I am here. I started fresh in Eastwatch and found almost immediate support."

Taf brimmed. "Good news. About time someone pushed for change." He leaned onto the table. "Tell me. How did you get around the Rights of the Privilege?"

"I rewrote the principles and appealed to adaptation within the new charter."

"Did you have to rewrite any of the acts?"

"Every. Single. One."

Taf stared off into the sky smeared with the bountiful colors of sunset. "Imagine the change. A Camoor being given a fair wage. I may not live to see that future, but I am glad to know it is less a dream that it once was."

Conversation mixed with wine and food. Time melted like the honey-flavored butter spread on the crusty brown toast that reminded Taf of home.

After a light meal of seasoned fish, he found himself walking beside Maisali between trimmed hedges crawling with silver vines. The colors of sunset were replaced by a night sky strewn with stars and patches of red and purple intermixing to make a section of deep blue. Night blooms were starting to show themselves among the hedges, the soft white petals opening up just enough to catch some starlight.

They used to walk this way every time. It was never the same when he went without her.

Taf turned to face her. In the silver hue of starlight, to call her beautiful would be an understatement to a degree he could not fathom. He stepped forward and reached to take her hand, to say something that needed to be said.

Taf retracted his hand.

"Is the truth that hard to say?" Maisali asked.

She took a step toward him.

His pulse quickened. What would he say? He had missed his chance five years ago.

"You were always too slow for my taste," said Maisali. "Come, we might as well enjoy the Gardens if we cannot enjoy the company."

Taf fell in line behind her and matched her stride. He felt his heart slow to a normal pulse, and for that, he was thankful.

"I never was much company. I blame my occupation for the lack of etiquette training."

"Can you imagine a group of soldiers attending one of the King's banquets?"

Taf laughed. "I can, and it is a disaster."

"I miss this."

"Me too. Stars, so many great memories. Do you remember when we argued over table settings?"

Maisali stopped and turned toward him but did not look up at him. "Taf, why..." She did not finish.

Taf reached out and took her hand. "Leave it. The past belongs to the past."

"No." Her voice shook. She stared daggers at him. "You owe me an explanation. I cannot leave it buried. The wound is still bleeding, Taf. What did you think would happen? Could you actually imagine me marrying some other noble and settling down?" Tears were starting to brim at the corners of her eyes.

Taf felt his heart twist. He hated seeing her like this. He wished he could make it so that she never felt pain ever again.

"I loved you," she said. Tears poured from her eyes.

Taf gathered her into his arms and let her tears stain his tunic.

He fought within himself until the warmth of his heart overcame the worry of his mind. "I still love you," he told her, softly.

"Then why did you let me walk away?" She wrapped her arms around him. "Why did you let me go?"

"Because I love you, and you deserve someone who can love you with a whole life. I would give you everything I can, but it is not enough."

Maisali pushed off his chest and looked at him. "You never asked me. We made a life of what we had already. What would make you think I needed, or wanted more?"

"You deserve—"

"You blundering fool," she interrupted, pulling her hands free and taking a step back. He missed her, a breath apart and he hated the absence.

Taf pulled out his pocket cloth and held it for her. She drew her own and used it instead.

"Taf, do you mean to tell me the only reason we never wed was because you were concerned that I would not be satisfied with a few nights together?"

"Yes," he said. The admission was sudden, and as soon as he gave it, the weight he had been holding for years vanished. In its place he felt all the foolishness of never being honest. "I sound a fool saying it now, but I did not want you to think that I cared any less for you. I have my duty to the crown, and if I was not attached, of course I would work an honest wage and be the husband you—"

She grabbed his face and kissed him on the mouth. Her wet, lips tasted better than he remembered. Taf wrapped a hand around her back and another around her neck. He pressed his lips deep into hers.

They pulled apart, and Taf felt his whole body sigh.

"Taf, you fool."

Taf let his head touch hers. He stared at the grass at his feet. The warmth of her hand wrapped in his and the presence of her company was better than anything else in all of Ta'Thaloon.

"I am a fool."

"I will take you regardless."

Taf lifted his head until they were staring deep into each other's eyes. "You—"

"Do. NOT. Ruin this. Let me speak and keep that beautiful mouth of yours shut." Maisali narrowed her eyebrows and got the look that told Taf there was no argument to be made. "I love you, as stupid as you can be, and I will take a life with you if it is only as often as you can spare. I promise I will never get in the way of your duty to King or Kingdom, but I demand that when you are not saving the world that you will give what time you have left so that I can treasure what we have rather than scraping scraps from memories that grow dimmer with the day."

"Is this a proper proposal?"

"You oaf," she said, hitting his chest.

Taf cupped her beautiful face and planted a kiss on her lips. He drew back, and their breath mingled in the night air. "I will have to think about it."

She pushed him away. Taf chuckled but stopped when she gave him the look. The silence between them grew cold.

Taf finally found his courage. "I have had nightmares about this moment. Of what the truth would cost me. Do you mean it?"

"Every word. Including you being stupid."

"Somehow I did not doubt that part." Taf felt himself pulled between excitement and intimidation. "This is too good to be true."

"Do not jinx this for me. Knowing my imagination, I am about to find out this is just another twisted dream and I have to wake up alone."

"Maisali. I am so sorry. If I had known that you—"

"What did I say about keeping that stupid, beautiful mouth shut?"

Taf stepped forward and wrapped her into his arms. "What did I ever do to deserve—"

"Taf. Say it."

"What?"

Maisali took his hands in hers. Her delicate skin looked out of place next to his gnarled, beaten hands. "I want you to look me in the eyes and tell me you will marry me."

"Yes. Wait. It was a proposal?" Taf frowned. "When we tell the story, can we make it so that I asked?"

"No."

Taf sighed. "What would I do without you?"

"What did you do without me?"

"Worked, I suppose. Wandered around town at times. I went on two dates. They were…disasters."

Maisali shook her head. "I could have told you that. Did you wear this," she motioned to his outfit, "both times?"

"Yes."

"What did you do without me? No wonder you did not have any other dates."

He thought he looked decent.

They continued their walk through the Gardens, hand in hand. It felt so right, to have her beside him.

Taf found himself taking her home down the same route they had taken so many times for so many years. They spoke softly about matters serious and solemn, nonchalant and jovial. Everything fit back into place so naturally it felt as if the years were nothing more than a lifting of a quill off the page of their story.

A light burned in the Law Keepers' office of High Town. Even on the night of festivals it was rare that the Law Keepers stayed past sunset. Grumbling morphed into angry shouts. Taf watched as the Law Keeper sergeant walked a man out of the office and motioned to the street.

Taf stiffened as he struggled to discern the motive behind the raised voices.

"Go on," Maisali said.

Taf turned to her. "What?"

"You want to know what the matter at hand is, correct?"

"Yes, but it does not seem to be a serious matter."

Maisali shook her head. "I meant what I said."

"About?"

"I will take what I can get and will not expect you to be any-one but yourself. Go and check in. Perhaps your many years can help solve their quarrel."

"We are on a date."

Maisali raised an eyebrow. "And what would you be thinking about all the way back to my home? I would have to drag you across the threshold if I wanted any more of you. Even then I have no guarantee."

"It should just be a moment."

"Come on then, save the world."

Taf and Maisali walked over to the dispute. Two Law Keepers

stood with arms crossed in front of a Camoor who looked to be in his middle years.

"Greetings," called Taf. He examined the Law Keepers as he approach. The sergeant was an old friend, Ghar, but the other younger man was not known to him.

"Fist of the King. Lady Maisali," said Ghar, bowing reverently. The young man fumbled to follow suit.

Ghar cleared his throat. "Apologies if we disturbed your evening with Lady Maisali."

Taf shook his head. "No bother. I only wanted to see if there is any way I can lend myself." He glanced at the Camoor to get a gauge of the man. There was nothing about his bearing that gave the impression of criminal activity. In fact, the Camoor looked the part of an honest man.

"Just a bit of a misunderstanding," said Ghar. He did not meet Taf's gaze. "To be honest, I raised my voice from frustration, nothing wrong done by this man."

"It's my doing," the Camoor told Taf. "Didn't meant to be any kind of bother."

"This man is a Fist of the King. You must address him—"

Taf raised his hand to silent Ghar. "Sergeant, this is not the court. I imagine this man has never had the privilege of formalities." He turned to the Camoor. "Call me Taf."

"Jatha," the man said, looking ashamed.

"What business brings you to High Town? Forgive my assumption, but I do not think you live here."

"No sir, of course not. I've come to ask about a captain. Of the ship I was on last time I took from port."

Ghar interjected. "He was knocking on doors asking after

the man in question."

"It takes confidence to ask after strangers. What has taken you so far afield?" Taf asked.

"My son," said Jatha.

"Taf," said Ghar. "I am afraid this is a simple matter. As I have been trying to instruct this man, children are not always as faithful as we would hope."

No, they are not, Taf thought. The reminder tasted bitter. Beside him Maisali looked distant. Perhaps they were both thinking of their intimate conversations about his fractured upbringing. She was one of the few to know his story.

"Not my son," Jatha insisted. "Not Jathalor. Boy isn't always keen on thinking what he's doing through and might get in a bit of trouble now and again."

"Taf, he is talking as if the boy has been taken or something of the sort."

"In Nathalem port?" Taf asked. "Do not mistake me. I am not foolish enough to think it does not happen."

Jatha shook his head side to side slowly, eyes downcast. "I don't know what happened. Don't think it was here either. Fever in the head put me in bed for the first few days of the voyage. Came to and Jathalor was gone. I was asking after the captain to see if he knew more."

"You have been home, to see first?"

"Yessir."

"Did you ask after his friends?"

Jatha nodded. "I didn't start here. No sir. Even asked about the port authority to see if something turned up. They be good about reporting the comings and goings of ships. They told me same as this here Law Keeper."

Ghar looked as if he was about to say something.

"I will see to the rest of the matter," Taf told them. Maybe it was a wasted effort, but he would not deny a father's love for his son if it could be helped. "Rest well and thank you for your service."

"King and Kingdom," said Ghar.

"King and Kingdom," Taf replied.

He, Lady Maisali, and Jatha walked a few paces away while the two Law Keepers headed back inside.

"No wonder you stirred the Keepers," said Taf. He chuckled. "Knocking on the doors of strangers past nightfall. Must have given a few people a start."

"More than one man threatened me with a good pair of boots."

Taf laughed. "What a sight." He settled his laugher when Jatha did not join in. He took a calm, quiet tone. "Let me be the first to add that it is not uncommon for boys to leave home."

I did, Taf thought. *And there was no home for me when I returned.*

Jatha looked him in the eyes. "I don't know how to assure you. I'd pledge my life that Jathalor didn't run from me. A mighty fine boy, and could make a good deck hand one day, but he's young and not always where he should be."

His son could have been poached by another captain on coming ashore. If the boy can work, it might be reason enough. If the son found labor in another port while the father was sick and the pay was better, who would blame him for taking what came?

"You've that look they all be giving me," Jatha said.

Taf met the man's gaze.

"I'll say this once more and be on my way, not wanting to take up the time of someone so important. Nor of you, miss.

We're all we got left in this life. No proper home or nothing. No wife or mother or sister or brother. Jathalor wouldn't leave me."

Taf saw in the eyes of this father all the love he never got from his own. It was enough to make him believe it, foolish as it may have sounded.

"Very well. I will see about the captain and ask him about your son."

Jatha frowned. "You'd do that?"

"I cannot promise I will find anything of consequence."

"You've no reason to help me."

"What is the purpose of serving the King if not to care for his people?"

Jatha stared at Taf. "I've no way to thank you. Give you the shirt off my back if I didn't think it'd be an insult."

Taf felt for the coin in his pocket and remembered the dirty little boy with the wide, honest eyes. *No insult.* "I will take the name of the captain and ship before we part."

"Captain Rora. He captains *The Second Sail.*"

"If I need to find you, where should I ask?"

"I'll be at port first light. Always am."

Taf laid a hand on the man's shoulder. "Stay safe on your way home and do not deny yourself the pleasure of a good night's rest. Take a drink or smoke if you need it. I will do what I can do for your boy."

Jatha headed down the street. Taf felt a hand touch his. Instincts kicked in and he reached for the sword at his side.

"Forgot about me, did you?"

Taf turned to Lady Maisali feeling a fool. "No, I—"

"Save your excuses." She took both his hands in hers. "I have not forgotten much of our conversations and none of your past. This seems to stir a certain sentiment for you."

"I thought those skeletons to be well buried."

She leaned forward and softly kissed him on the lips. "Some of the past is still present."

Taf smiled. "I have missed you."

"You must at least walk me home before you see after this boy. I want you to know I expect you to keep me updated on the matter. Jatha certainly believed what he was saying."

"A good father."

Taf started their walk, head swimming with considerations. What if the boy had been taken? What did it mean? The King spoke truth when he said the realm was sick.

"Will you be able to find time for me tomorrow?" asked Maisali.

Taf returned his focus to the moment and the woman who wanted him despite himself. It was too wonderful to be believed. "I will do everything I can to make time for you."

It was not long before they were standing at the door. Taf held her hands in his. "Maisali," he started, struggling for words. He could not remember the last time his heart felt so full.

"I know," said Maisali. She smiled. Stars, he had missed her smile. "I do hope you stay safe as you interrogate captains."

Taf furrowed his eyebrows. "Interrogate. Do you think I am going to march to his door tonight and demand an answer?"

"That does sound like something you would do."

"I will have you know I have learned a bit about nobles. Disturbing a nobleman at this time of night will only put him on edge."

"You are going to get him drunk."

Taf frowned. "How did you know?"

"It is what I would do to get answers. Especially if there is something criminal involved. Besides, the only wisdom you ever learned was mine to teach."

Taf had no argument.

"Taf, are you telling me you are showing restraint?"

"Only in small measure. Let us not pretend I am not going to be about finding out before first light."

Lady Maisali gave him a soft smile. "I would expect nothing else. You will call on me tomorrow, if you find the time?"

"I will make every effort." Taf swallowed the lump in his throat. "Is that to say our date is concluded?"

"You are not the only one with labors in the morning."

Taf nodded. "Of course, you are right."

"Taf."

He looked up. The light framed her face perfectly. "I expect my kiss goodnight."

Taf took her waist in his hand and stepped close enough to feel the warmth of her breath. "I missed you," he told her. "More than I realized."

"Do not miss me now," said Maisali. "I am right here."

A NOSE FOR TROUBLE

BRAERON FELT HIS FACE getting hot. "Do you think I've never worked before? I've known cattle get a better wage for their labors."

"This is standard pay," the mercenary captain told him. He was graying with a large forehead and mean scowl. If it weren't for him being captain of the best company in town, Braeron would let him know just how ugly he was.

The stupid-looking man sitting next to the captain kept his eyes narrowed and jaw set. His arms were thick and his hair a greasy, tangled mess. "What kind of cattle get a wage?"

Braeron rolled his eyes. "I'll prove myself any way you want me to. I know I look young, but I've been through the depths of Ta'Thaloon and back. Spent a few years in the military too, which I think might've been worse."

The mercenary captain crossed his arms. "That's a lot of talk, boy."

Braeron put both hands on the table. He looked the man dead in the eye. "I'm no boy, sir."

The captain pushed back his chair and stood up. He was as tall as Braeron and clad in full half-plate. "I'll call you whatever I want to. You'd be lucky if I took you on as a maid."

Braeron spat to the side. "You're missing out, you are. I'm not just some stone-stupid sellsword like most of your company."

"Is he insulting me?" asked the large, greasy-haired mercenary.

"I believe he is. Would you care to show him the door?" the captain asked.

"I'd be more like to show him a boot."

The captain settled back in his chair. "Do what you want."

Braeron watched the greasy-haired mercenary rise. He was a head taller than Braeron and built like a small tree. Stupid, yes. Strong, impossibly so. He suddenly remembered Catear and wrestled with a bout of unexpected guilt.

He side-stepped the large man's attempt to grab his arm. "I'll see myself out," Braeron grumbled.

Braeron headed through the crowded tavern, dodged an incoming patron, and slipped through the door out into the cool night air. *Not even a drink. Waste of my time.* He gritted his teeth to keep from screaming his rage. He wasn't so young or so foolish. Why was it so hard to find decent gold?

He stalked around the side of the bustling tavern and turned the corner, checking twice to make sure the captain hadn't sent someone to chase him off. He plopped himself down on the ground. Thoughts started to mix into a pungent stew of emotions. He leaned his head back and stared up into the cloudy night sky.

I should have just taken the job back in Halfway. The pay would've been terrible, but it would be a steady job. The kind his father took. Not much, but enough to leave a family wanting more.

Braeron sighed. Settling down to something easy tasted too much like failure. Besides, the last word he got from home was that his sister Cailie was getting married. A brand-new dress from Halfway was the talk of the town. That grand amount of gold came from working for the Crimson Briars. *Easy money is never easy.*

Maybe I should just go home. He would be able to see his brother grow and his sister start her family. He didn't even know the man she was to marry. Was she moving to Halfway? Mother would start talking about him needing to find a wife.

"I need a drink," he mumbled to himself, pushing off the ground with a grunt.

Braeron froze. Two men stood before him. Both were clean-cut, well dressed. The taller one was starting to gray and show crow's feet, but the other could only be ten or so years older than himself.

"Evening, officers." Braeron swallowed. "No trouble here. If loitering be a problem, it's to be no longer. About to mosey on my way to find a drink. Someplace else, that is."

Neither of them said a word. Was the mercenary captain connected with the Law Keepers? *Stars, this is just my luck.*

"I mean no offense by what I said to that sir just a few moments ago. I'll be the first to tell you I lose my head a bit. Seeing red is useful when it counts but not so much when we get to talking. Just a bit of a misunderstanding."

They watched him like a hawk does a young rabbit. The bird doesn't wait because it is afraid it will miss the small animal. It waits because it can. Because it wants to savor the moment.

"Stars above! What is this about? I've done nothing illegal. Maybe started a few fights. Not exactly made friends with some of the fellows during service. If this be about me working for them Briars, I'll tell you I quit soon as I knew who and what they were."

The taller one pounced, grabbing Braeron by the shirt and hoisting him into the air. The officer slammed Braeron against the wall.

"Where is the boy?" the officer asked in an even tone.

Braeron bit back the strong-worded rebuke that first came to mind. He grabbed the man's wrist and tried to twist himself free. "Let go. Stupid, witless mutt. I've done nothing wrong."

"Not much control," said the shorter man. He studied Braeron with a calculating grimace.

"Where is the boy?"

"What boy?" asked Braeron, dropping his arms. The officer was far stronger than he expected, especially considering his age.

"Taf, let him down."

The taller man, Taf, looked over at the other officer. "I am afraid he might poke me." He still dropped Braeron.

Braeron fought to get his shirt back in order before looking at the officer. "Did you hear the part about my service? I happen to know which end of a sword, or dagger, to stick a man with."

"Is that a threat?"

Braeron bit his tongue. "No, sir."

"Worked for the Briars, did you?"

"Just a bit here and there. Never really talked about being a part of their merry little band of brigands. Found myself in the midst of a kidnapping and told them I wanted out. They didn't want to use words."

"So you were involved?"

Braeron gave an incredulous look at Taf. "What have I just

said? I've no part in that. Thought it was work, same as the sort I find for myself here and again."

"He is a mercenary, Taf."

"Arma, I do not think he is just a coinsword. It sounds like he has played the part of a criminal."

Braeron looked between the two men. "Am I not using the right words? I was their captive for the better part of three weeks before I wiggled my way out. Well, burned my way out."

Arma, the younger officer, stepped forward. He was not as intimidating as Taf, but his eyes were sharp. "You mistake us. We are concerned about a young Camoor. He was working the docks here a few days past."

Braeron looked from one officer to the next. What were they doing asking after a Camoor? There were hundreds working the port.

He let out a long breath. "I've not the slightest—"

Taf interrupted him in a stern tone that bordered on rage. "You were last seen with the boy in question. Walking across the docks long past sunset."

Braeron felt the memory surface. The young Camoor who reminded him of Jakoron.

"Oh, Jathalor. There's a fellow who needs a bit of luck. Never could be in the right place at the right time."

"Where. Is. He?"

"I walked him to his ship. Watch him board under the watch of the captain. That there captain looked redder than me. Told the boy I would vouch for him. He told me the trouble was past and I could go my way. I watched him board the ship under the watch of that there captain."

Taf eased up on Braeron. He turned to the other officer and whispered something about the captain.

Braeron checked to see if he could slip away. Whatever was going on, he needed out. Trouble with the law was best avoided. Taf watched his every move out of the corner of his eye. So much for finding work tonight.

"We will need to hear your telling of that night," Taf said, crossing his arms.

Braeron scuffed the packed dirt beneath his feet with his right foot. "Course I'll say as much as needs to be said. I might be willing to say a bit more if you'd buy me a drink. Or two."

"A drink for a story is a fair trade. Come on then, we may still have labors left this night." Taf headed to the corner as if he intended to get the drink inside.

"Hold there, remember me telling the part about causing trouble."

"It seems to be a common theme for you."

Arma looked over at Taf. "We could just buy the drink for him inside and see how badly he wants it."

"That'd be a mighty cruel thing to do," said Braeron.

Taf shrugged. "Sounds fair to me."

"Come now. Don't you want to hear about my work with the Briars? I did mention they were at the work of taking people."

"One drink," said Taf.

Braeron gave them his most dashing smile. An idea came to mind and he allowed himself to entertain it. "Won't be wasted neither. I've just the place in mind. It will be a bit of a walk seeing as the other closer tavern and I had a falling-out the night before last."

"You certainly make an impression," Arma said.

Braeron led them away from the docks proper and farther into town. Braeron kept the pace even so they could follow but gave himself a few steps ahead. He'd take an easy out if it presented itself.

They walked through the empty streets of Port Gregorious. A few lights burned but it wasn't enough to keep the shadows from feeling deep and menacing. He led them northeast, out of the town proper and on a dirt track. The two Keepers followed, but he could tell they were skeptical. They should be, as this was the shady part of town, and if he played his cards right a perfect chance for him to escape.

They reached their destination. The drinking hole may have once been a tavern, but it was no longer. There was one room with lots of chairs and tables crammed together like salted fish. The bread was good and the ale better than the piss most other places served. Even this early in the week, the place was sure to be packed with all sorts of people.

Everyone turned to the door when the two officers walked in. Braeron smiled to himself and maneuvered around the room until he found a few chairs and a small table in the far corner. He took a seat with his back facing the kitchen.

"Braeron," called Raile. The young woman set a stein of ale in front of him and leaned close enough to whisper. "Why'd you bring them here?"

"Having a drink is all."

"Better keep it that way. No need for nonsense. I'm busy enough as it is." She was cute, the kind of face he loved watching smile. They'd shared a few drinks and enough memories for him to feel bold.

Braeron leaned back. "When do you get off? I've a mind to show up late for work tomorrow."

"You wish." Raile gave him a sly smile. "Your friends be drinking the same?"

"I've not the slightest."

"Not friends?"

The officers joined them. Arma gave Raile an awkward dip of the head joined with a "miss." Taf walked over to where Raile was standing and reached over Braeron and grabbed the stein.

Taf took a long drink. He gave the stein's contents an appraising look. "That is not a bad drop." He leaned over to Raile and whispered something before slipping something into her hand.

"Course, sir." Raile vanished.

Braeron watched Taf take a seat and chug the rest of the ale. This wasn't standard military.

Raile appeared moments later, dropping drinks off for all three of them before melding into the madness. Braeron studied the room. Two tables were paying and leaving. Three kept glancing over at the officers.

"I think we may need to speak with the captain again," said Taf.

Arma took a long drink from his stein. "I doubt we would get more out of him."

"There is more to this than we know. Killing people is more what I would expect from the Briars."

"What would they gain? The price for a slave cannot be worth the trouble. Where would they even find a buyer? Far to the north?"

"Or far enough south."

Arma moved his stein back and forth by the handle. He'd

not even had a sip of the drink. "I do not see the profits."

"What about motive? Why would they start taking people?"

"The better question is *what*. What does someone do with captives?"

Taf leaned forward. The two officers continued the discussion in harsh, hushed whispers.

Braeron drank and let himself ease into the seat. As his mind settled, he thought about the Briars caging people. Seemed someone would need to be paying through the nose for souls.

The reality of why the men were here settled into his stomach. Jathalor was missing. He'd let the boy go to the ship without a word, and now he was gone. Braeron didn't even want to think about the drink in front of him now. If he'd known, he would have fought the entire crew for the boy. What kind of monster would take a little boy prisoner?

"You need to move. Preferably out the door and into a freshly dug hole."

Braeron planted his feet and gripped the chair with one hand. A brutish man with a curly mustache loomed over Taf and Arma. The man kept a hand on a piece of naked steel hanging at his hip.

Taf frowned up at the man. "Arma, are we still within the King's borders?"

"Last I checked."

"Man has a right to drink and eat where he pleases. Is that not the law?"

"Last I checked."

The ruffian wrapped his hand around the hilt of his sword. "I asked nicely already. I won't do it again."

Braeron scooted his chair until he had a straight shot toward the kitchen.

Taf looked over at Arma. "He did ask nicely."

The tension in the room grew until Braeron stuttered a few gulps of air. *Please, just leave.*

Taf stood up and chugged the rest of his stein. "Stars, that is good ale." He smashed the empty mug against the ruffian's head.

The ruffian hit the ground with a loud thud. The whole room grew uncomfortably silent.

"That was a bit excessive," said Arma.

All around the room, patrons pushed back their chairs and rose to their feet. Knives, short swords, and clubs were drawn and brandished.

"Maybe not enough," Taf said.

Braeron flew toward the kitchen. The room behind him erupted into a cacophony of scraping chair legs and shifting tables. Raile was standing and staring through the open door. Braeron put a hand on her upper back.

"Don't know if I'll be let back in after this," he said.

"Don't know if I'll have a job."

The two officers were standing back-to-back, swords drawn, and feet planted in standard military style. Maybe it wouldn't come to steel.

Raile turned away. "I don't think I've the stomach to watch. Let's be away." He felt his hand slip off her back.

Braeron started to turn to follow her. A prick of guilt unsettled his nerves and stopped his legs from going any farther. *Not my fight*, he told himself. But he had brought them here. The two officers weren't harming anyone. They were looking for a boy

Braeron should have protected.

He turned himself around. The room was pressing in on the two officers. The two men slashed and blocked with practiced ease but they were outnumbered ten to one. Tonight was about finding work, not causing trouble.

Braeron hurried over to the two officers. A battle song rose inside of him. He felt fear, excitement, and a tangible desire to test his metal. He'd always felt at home with his sword drawn.

He picked up his overturned chair and swung it across his body. The wood smashed into the closest ruffians, splintering with an audible crack.

Another ruffian swung a short sword at his midsection. Braeron stepped back and unsheathed his sword. He dodged the next swing. Braeron drove the sword into the ruffian's leg. The man roared, stumbling back.

A ruffian wielding a sizable club swung at Braeron's head. He adjusted his footing but was too slow. A hand yanked him backward, out of the way of the incoming cudgel.

"You need to watch your footwork," said Taf. He swung his sword into an incoming blow, blocking the attack and sending the man stumbling to the side. "If you are going forward, keep one of your feet pivoted. Preferably your dominant foot."

Arma battered a man back into the crowd. "He means the foot you usually advance with."

A few of the men were fleeing out the door, leaving the crowd of ruffians a tad slimmer but still fat with red-faced rage.

"Crossbow," said Taf.

Braeron found the weapon raised and pointed at Taf. *What have I gotten myself into?*

The twang of the string snapping back mixed with the thud of the bolt finding its target.

Taf held an overturned table in front of him. The point of the crossbow bolt protruded through the bottom.

"Make it count," said Taf.

Taf charged forward; Arma hurried behind with sword drawn. One of the ruffians got too close and earned himself a quick death. A large, muscled man wielding a mean club charged Arma's back.

Braeron rushed forward, driving his weapon into the ruffian's back before he could reach Arma. Braeron felt the steel sink deep into the man's flesh. He yanked the sword free and faced his next enemy.

Braeron deflected an incoming dagger and sent the man back with a flourish of his blade.

The man at Braeron's feet moaned. Blood stained the floor and colored the man's shirt a splotchy crimson. Braeron watched as the man's eyes rolled back into his head. An alien feeling crept into his bones. He had killed a man. Drove him through. Ended his life. Braeron felt sick to his stomach.

Arma shoved Braeron to the side to engage another enemy. Taf cut down the crossbow wielder.

The thud of an overturned chair joined the sound of the stampede of feet headed for the door. Arma stood next to Braeron, crimson blade held at the ready.

"I cannot believe this," said Taf. He stepped over to where Braeron stood. "To think men would kill Law Keepers this close to Nathalem."

"King is right," Arma said. "Something is stirring in the hearts of men."

"A wicked breeze." Taf shoved his sword down in front of a ruffian who rolled over. The man looked up at Taf with wide eyes. "Wait right there. I have questions."

Arma held out a hand for Braeron. "Steady."

The world felt like the sea, swaying up and down, up and down. "Going be sick."

Taf stepped up and looked Braeron in the eyes. "I would have thought you would have bled your green during service."

"I was too young," said Braeron. He felt his stomach churn upside downside and around. "Took me off the lines when they learned. I've left men to bleed, had one drown, but this—" The image of the dying man's empty eyes flashed to mind.

Taf nodded his understanding. "Get to the kitchen if you need to empty your stomach. Bad form to do it among the dead."

"And dying," added Arma.

Braeron swallowed the bile and breathed out slowly. "I'll manage." He felt his stomach start to bubble again.

"No shame in it," Taf told him. "I can still remember the first time I ended a life. Not a small matter."

Braeron rushed for the kitchen. He made it just inside and threw up the contents of his stomach onto the floor. He dropped to his knees and retched until he had nothing left to give, and then he spit burning bile.

He walked back, wiping his mouth with the back of his hand. He felt resolved but oddly empty.

Taf and Arma were standing in front of the unfortunate survivor. The man was tied to a chair.

"You mentioned working for the Briars," said Taf. He motioned to the tattoo just above the ruffian's elbow.

Braeron examined the work. It wasn't something he knew for sure, but it looked like the thug wasn't an official part of the crew. The men he was caged by all had a rose at the top of their markings. This man's ink was only of twisted thorns and some strange script.

"Just a footpad, I would guess," said Braeron.

"Hopefully he knows enough to give us a bearing," Arma said.

Taf nodded, rolling up his sleeves while watching the Briar. He glanced over at Braeron. "Glad you came back," the officer said.

Braeron felt his chest swell with pride. "Welcome. Figured I couldn't leave two fine men to die."

"He means for your sake," Arma said.

"What do you mean?"

Taf yanked the rope holding the Briar in place. "We thought you brought us here to get us killed. If you did not come back it would be you sitting in this chair. Once we hunted you down."

Braeron felt the blood leave his face. He stuttered to find a good answer. He wasn't one of them. Of course he wasn't. He risked his life to leave the criminals.

Braeron pulled back his right sleeve. "I've no marks on me beside what I got from service."

Taf turned to face him. The officer didn't look down at the mark dating Braeron's official enlistment and service level. He looked Braeron dead in the eyes. "Men make judgments from what they can see, but it is our choices that define us."

Arma stepped up to the Briar. He grabbed the man's hair and pulled his head back. "Taf," Arma said. "It appears that he is going into shock."

The Briar started to twitch. His mouth foamed and his eyes rolled back into his head. Moments later the stillness and silence declared the man dead.

"Stars," Taf grumbled. "Now we need to hunt down another one."

Braeron considered the room. Eight dead. Tables and chairs lay broken and distorted. He picked his way across the battlefield, methodically checking the dead for their marks. Braeron turned over the man he had slain with his own hand. Seeing the man's face brought an uncomfortable bout of nausea. Braeron swallowed the mouthful of bile and rolled back the man's sleeve.

The sprawling ink contained a rose. Braeron checked the pockets, painfully aware of the fact he was disgracing the dead. Even on the battlefield, he never did enjoy picking plunder. A thought came to mind. When they first took him captive, they took his shirt and turned it inside out as if he might have something hidden.

Braeron probed the shirt with one hand under and the other over. If he was to have a secret pocket it would be—Braeron found the extra stitching. At least what was left of it.

He cut away the shirt and used a dagger to tear through the seams of the stitching until the hidden pocket opened enough for him to pull free the page. Red soaked the paper all the way through. Braeron slowly peeled the pages apart from each other until he could confirm that between his sword's damage and the dead man's blood there was no hope of learning anything.

Taf took the page from Braeron. He walked over to one of the tables.

"Braeron, get me a lantern or candle from the kitchen. I need an open flame."

Braeron weaved through the wreckage and into the kitchen. He found an old lantern in one of the cabinets and oil in another. He lit a piece of kindling from the dying flames inside the hearth. He burned the wick until it took the light.

He carried the burning lantern back to where the two men were talking in low, hushed voices. Braeron looked to the door which was barely hanging on by one of its hinges. What if the Briars came back? And with more men?

"Perhaps we should relocate," said Braeron. "Not sure I want to tangle with the Briars again."

Taf took the lantern and placed it on the table. "Stand here." He motioned to a place around the table.

Braeron turned away from the door and did as instructed, watching the flame flicker as it continued to burn with endless hunger. Taf grabbed his shoulder and pulled him close until his shadow covered the blood-soaked page lit by the fire below.

Taf moved the stained page forward and back, adjusting the angle and twisting it to the side until he stopped and started to mouth words sporadically. Braeron didn't read well. His mother would hate to hear him admit it. She tried; stars know she tried.

"A ledger?" Arma asked aloud. "Shipping manifests with the name of the ships and captains."

Braeron thought about the captain who might be responsible for Jathalor's disappearance. "It'd let us know which captains are working with the Briars."

Taf continued to look over the page. Braeron could barely see anything from the angle. Not that there was much to look at. Just a mess of red splotches atop small squiggles. His eyes fell on something in the bottom corner. A strange symbol that seemed familiar. He had seen it, hadn't he? The memory mocked him from the edges of his mind, telling him he should know it but never letting him have the satisfaction of seeing it.

Taf handed the page to Arma. "We will need to send word to keep a lookout for these captains."

Arma carefully folded the page and slid it into his shirt. "This may need to involve the Shadow Council."

"No wonder the King was so quick to send us after the boy. Men willing to sell people like cattle; what could convince a man to do such a thing?"

"The buyer must be setting an exorbitant price. The Kingdom is not as healthy as I hoped."

"Lady Maisali will want to hear about the matter."

Arma looked over at Taf with an expression that neared mockery. "Make sure to include the heroic retelling of charging across the room like a battering ram."

"It worked, did it not?"

"I was not belittling your efforts."

"Just mocking my recklessness."

Arma smiled. It was the first time he had even cracked a grin, and it looked strange on his usually cold demeanor. "I am simply attempting to help you with your court affairs."

"I will have you know that Lady Maisali has been tasked with overseeing our operation from the court."

Braeron's brain kept rolling over the picture. He couldn't place it but it was there. He stepped between the two men. "Can I see the page? Might be I know something I just can't remember."

Arma interjected. "What are your thoughts, Taf?"

Taf crossed his arms and looked over Braeron the same way

his father did when he thought Braeron had done something wrong. "This is King's business. I am still unsure whether you can be trusted."

"Found it, didn't I?"

Arma handed the page to Braeron but Taf grabbed Braeron's arm before he could take the paper. "Burn it, and I will strap you to the chair."

Braeron carefully unfolded the blood-spattered page and used the light to make sense of it. The mark in the right-hand corner was a bunch of squiggly lines in a weird shape with a phrase inscribed in the middle of the symbol.

The memory snapped into focus. This was the same marking on the door to the tomb where Catear had died. There was only one person who would be using the marks.

"I know who is using this mark," said Braeron.

"How sure are you?"

Braeron folded the page and handed it back to Arma. How confident was he? The memory replayed in such vivid detail he could taste the sweat and fear stuck in his throat as he ran from the monstrosity of flesh and metal.

"Sure as the sun."

"I suppose that solves at least one matter," said Taf. "Have you anything stashed about? We need to prepare to leave as soon as we have our heading."

"What're you getting at?" Braeron asked.

Arma put the page away. "You are coming with us."

"If this is a discussion of work, we will need to talk gold."

Taf stepped forward and looked Braeron in the eyes. "You are coming with us because I am not yet convinced you have not played a part. I would rather know where you are if you plan on stabbing me in the back."

Braeron had nothing to say in his defense. *Trouble with the law.* He sighed.

Taf straightened up and pulled out a rag to clean off his sword. He faced Arma. "We will need to comb the area for the Briars. We need to rouse the Keepers. If there is a hideout here, I want it found."

"Agreed," Arma said.

Braeron followed the two men as they headed for the door. At least he had work, of sorts.

DINNER FOR ONE

KALLIOM PRODUCED THE KEY to his personal wine cellar. It had been almost a year since he last opened the vault. Tonight's dinner was exactly the right occasion to celebrate with a good vintage.

He unlocked the door and opened it, revealing a staircase that headed into the cool damp cellar. Kalliom took the stairs carefully with the lantern before him. He slid the key into his pocket and started to twist the ring on his right middle finger back and forth. It was a strange habit, but it helped keep his nerves in check.

Tonight, Haili would be coming to dine in his home. Most of their dates had been at her small apartment situated on the eastern wing of the library. He did not often let anyone into his home. It was his sanctuary away from all the nonsense of politics and antics of academia.

They had seen each other for longer than he had anticipated. She was brilliant and a great conversationalist. He never felt like he needed to hide the nuances of his learning from her. Previous relationships usually reached a breaking point where learning needed to stay within the confines of school.

Haili was different. He had thought her a distraction, but she morphed into a confidante and friend. Relationships changed with time. He knew plenty of couples who enjoyed each other's company enough and never discussed the reality of what they were doing until one day they woke up and found themselves miserably married.

"This one," he said aloud, proud of himself for remembering where he put it. The cellar consisted of rows and rows of bottles held at a slight angle to ensure their viability. This particular bottle was a gift from the King of Nathalem after his research on a project associated with stabilizing the flow of the waterways and ensuring minimal corrosion of the foundation. It still baffled him that someone was foolish enough to build a city on top of a river.

Kalliom smiled to himself as he handled the fifty-year-old bottle. The label was a beautiful script with flowers covering the edges. He had once visited the vineyard which rested on a hill about an afternoon's journey from Nathalem. The ground was rich with minerals. It may have been a seabed at one time.

He headed up the stairs, then shut and locked the door before heading to the table. Normally he would have a Camoor overseeing every aspect of the dinner, but tonight was special. Of course, he had someone making the meal. He was not to be degraded to that, but he set the table and chose the flowers.

Kalliom opened the bottle and poured it into a stunning crystal carafe. While the wine breathed, he headed into his study and through the door into his personal laboratory. His Alchemy set was steaming from something unassociated with the evening.

He did check to make sure the fat, brown leaves were still being properly distilled.

In the corner, inside a locked cupboard, was what he came for. Kalliom held the small bottle out and gently rocked it to make sure the contents were evenly distributed. This poison was his own creation and something he honestly did not expect to discover. It had stumbled into his lap while he was tinkering with tinctures.

Kalliom slid the bottle of poison into his pocket and headed out to ensure the cook was not making too much of a mess with his kitchen. Satisfied that the Camoor's efforts would be sufficient, Kalliom checked the time by the window overlooking the ocean. The sun was hanging low but not yet gracing the horizon.

He settled in at his desk and perused his patients' case notes. Three were dead as of yesterday. He checked over the dosage amounts for each and ensured that the others were receiving a variation. Every death gave him information, but he wanted better results. That was the difficulty with what he was attempting. In order to enslave a being into perfect subjugation it required they be dead, otherwise the will would get in the way. However, they needed to be alive enough to function and not start rotting. Cai'Tallai had managed to accomplish it in some form or fashion.

A knock on the door drew his attention from the case notes about a young Camoor who was proving to be especially stubborn. The boy was not yet dead but showed almost no progress in terms of mental instability.

Kalliom sorted his desk and headed for the door to greet Haili. His thoughts drifted to recent memories with her. He glanced at the table on his way.

He reached for the door but hesitated. *I almost forgot.* Kalliom opened the vial and dumped the contents into the wine. He watched the solution bubble and fizz before evaporating.

He opened the door for a pleasant-looking Haili.

"Good evening," she said, stepping in and handing him a basket.

Kalliom eyed the wicker. "Did you craft something for me?"

"Do not be silly, I had one of the Camoors from the kitchen make that. She owed me a favor."

Kalliom opened the top of the basket.

"It is a tart filled with cream and fruit jam," said Haili. "I figured a dessert would be fitting. Tonight is, after all, a special occasion."

"Speaking of special occasions." Kalliom turned around and poured them both a glass of wine. He handed her the crystal. "To the next step of your academic achievements."

Haili raised her glass and clinked the edge with his. "To the future."

Kalliom watched her about to take a sip while he drank enough to taste. It would be slow. She might not even notice a change the first few days.

"Oh," said Haili, setting down the glass.

Kalliom nearly spilled his wine on himself.

"I brought the formulas that you sent me," she said. Haili took a seat and produced several pages which she proceeded to stack beside her salad fork.

Kalliom regained his composure and took a seat at the table.

"I have to say, Cai'Tallai was certainly unprecedented in his approach to experimentation. One of the aspects I noticed in my current studies is how often 'modern' discovery is founded and

146

necessitated by previous information. As if we want to repeat knowledge instead of attempting to find something new. You show me a side of genius exemplified by Cai'Tallai by willingly starting with the unknown to discover the unknown."

Kalliom enjoyed the stroking of his ego. He took a sizable drink of wine. The opening was softer than he expected, and then it moved to the sides of his mouth with a touch of bitterness accented by spice. He stifled a cough. There was the poison. Good thing she hadn't drunk any yet.

"Are you well?"

"Fine. I forgot how to drink for a moment is all. Shall we begin?" asked Kalliom, dabbing his lips with his lap cloth.

"Please. I find myself excited to see what courses you chose for the evening."

Kalliom rang the bell beside his soup spoon. The Camoor emerged from the kitchen with two small plates. She set the food down in front of them at the same time and retreated to her labors. The salad was a collection of greens, nuts and fruit, all tossed in oil with a hint of citrus.

The food was acceptable.

"How do you intend to process your considerations?" asked Haili. She ate heartily but with enough dignity to spare any judgment. "I checked to ensure that your formulas were plausible, as you requested, but I doubt any of it will matter without the ability to study reactions."

Sharing his discovery and experiments would be a helpful means of processing some of his failed attempts, but he needed to ensure the word did not spread anywhere close to the council. What the twelve learned needed to be carefully fabricated.

"What would be your recommendation?" Kalliom asked, deflecting the question.

Haili finished her salad and reached for the wine. Kalliom watched, fork filled with an assortment of greens, suspended between his plate and mouth. She took up the glass of water instead and drank.

"To be honest, the best use would be on people. Animals are a fine basis, but the intricacies of our minds are too different from those of the beasts. Besides, you know this well, there are unexplainable aspects of the will that cause havoc during testing."

"Well said. If only there were a means of safely testing."

The plates were taken, and the next course brought. This was a green soup that smelled heavily of spices. Kalliom ate a spoonful and found the balance of savory and heat to be better than he had expected. He continued to eat while awaiting Haili's response.

"What if you were to use patients already at death's door? It may be a bit of an ethical dilemma, but you would find willing volunteers. Gold for those who will be left mourning and knowledge for those still alive."

Kalliom nodded while thinking about how he would go about processing that paperwork. Not many in the council would consider it a proper means of experimentation. Then again, if they knew what he was doing now they would call him a criminal and probably have him executed. Thus, the wine.

It was a shame. Haili was bright, knowledgeable, and willing to do what was necessary. He never actually discussed the possibility with his beneficiary, but Haili would make a useful addition to his research. What if there was a way to bring her into the fold? He would need to ensure she would keep the information close. Granted, she hadn't yet told anyone about their romantic involvement despite the fact Kalliom was certainly one of the most accomplished scholars of their day. *Soon to be of history.* It showed incredible self-control not to boast about being with him.

"Enough discussion about plausibility," said Haili. "After all, I am only musing. How are you testing?"

Kalliom took a drink of wine. The poison was not even noticeable anymore, or the alcohol was working on his head.

"Sewer rats," he said, spooning his last bit of soup.

"Camoor?" Haili asked.

Kalliom almost dropped his spoon.

"I am only teasing you. Of course you would not experiment on people so early on in the process. Granted, the rats of Nathalem would be the best source. No one would miss them. They are more of a strain on the population than a blessing."

Kalliom settled his thoughts. "The council would not be pleased, even if the logic is sound."

"Which is why you are experimenting with rats." She said it in a way that made him feel as if she conceded to what he said but believed more.

Haili reached for her wine. He would miss her. She was brilliant and willing to make sacrifices that others were not. He would have at most two days to pick her brain about formulas. *I could give her the antidote.* But his employer was very specific in her instructions. 'Kill her but keep suspicion low.' He did not want to end up being the one she decided was no longer useful.

Haili moved her arm out of the way of the Camoor taking the plate. She threw the woman a judgmental glare before lifting the wine to her lips.

The poison would be slow. If he understood correctly, the corrosion would start in the brain and slowly eat away at the soft flesh therein until the body was no longer able to cope with the lack of guidance. Then, well, the body would fail. Without the mind, there would nothing to hold it together.

"Oh," said Haili, setting down her untouched wine.

The Camoor served each of them a rack of lamb seasoned and lightly breaded. Steam rolled off the meat. The rest of the plate consisted of a melody of braised vegetables covered in dark seasoning and resembling burnt toast.

"I love lamb! How did you know? Kalliom, this is turning out to be quite an enjoyable dinner."

Kalliom started to twist one of his rings back and forth. He needed her to drink, but if she did not maybe he could explain to his employer...but what? *How would you convince her?* Kalliom knew she would not listen to him. She would not care, and his life would be forfeit.

He pulled the antidote from his pocket and uncorked it with one hand. He would get her to drink, somehow. Kalliom poured the antidote onto the ground before sliding the empty vial into his pocket.

"For you, I would gather the moons and the stars," he said.

Haili held her fork just above her plate. The meat was dripping grease, steam rolling up before evaporating into vapor so thin he could not see it. "Do you mean that?"

Kalliom smiled. "I do. You have been the companion I have been looking for my whole life." It was easy to say because it was the truth.

The meal was well seasoned and cooked. The vegetables were

surprisingly tasty. Kalliom amused himself by scraping off the seasoning on a carrot and examining the bits and pieces to guess the balance and process.

"I am curious," said Haili, pushing her plate a bit in front of her, most of it untouched. "How did you determine the means to distill Cai'Tallai's findings into usable formulas?"

"Therein lies the problem I currently face," Kalliom said. "As of now, the rats are responding so diversely that I have a hard time determining any root factors that can be used to help guide my research."

"I may be able to help with that." Haili handed him the stack of pages. "I noticed quite a few trends in the formulas that you wanted me to consider. You may have overlooked it while you were busy creating a wide base of conditions, but there is a foundation for each of the tinctures."

Kalliom gathered the pages and started to read through the formulas and considerations she had added. Her handwriting was precise with just enough feminine flair to distinguish it from his boring script. Most of her observations were those he gathered while double checking his work, but something stood out.

"You consistently have hirabatus circled." The common flower was often called Red Leaf and used in many teas and infusions. He used it because if boiled to a certain temperature and distilled in water, it turned to a weak alcohol.

Haili chewed on her most recent forkfull, covering her mouth and giving him an apologetic expression. Her cheeks lifted when she smiled and it pulled at her eyes in the cutest way. Kalliom lost himself for a moment in her natural beauty.

Haili swallowed and dabbed her face with her lap cloth. "You use hirabatus in every solution thus far, but if you notice, the level to which it is used is inconsistent. I think you may be distilling them at different levels as well."

"Yes. It was the cheapest option to ensure the solutions would last longer than a few days, but other ingredients produce alcohol in the process. I wanted to ensure I did not dilute the final solution."

She left her side of the table and walked around until she stood next to him. He had not noticed it before, but she smelled of sandalwood. It was his favorite scent.

"If you look here," she said, motioning to the list of ingredients on the right hand side of the page, "you will see that you do not account for hirabatus. I think you need to consider that it may be reacting with the process."

"Red leaf does nothing other than give poor men hangovers or make a boring tea."

"These solutions are unique."

Kalliom nodded. "I checked to ensure there was no record in any of the histories that accounts for the use of gil-vaine and deadroot."

"What if hirabatus is the primary cause of change?"

"It is nothing more than a base. Holding fluid. I do vary the distillation process—" Kalliom saw her wisdom the moment he started to talk about it. "The variation leaves some of the base material still in place. Even though it should not react, it may be causing contingencies I did not plan for."

Kalliom set the pages down, gathered Haili's face in his hands, and kissed her. She pressed into him. He wrapped an arm around her head and back.

"How could I have not seen that?" Kalliom asked.

"Even the brightest men need a woman to guide them," said Haili.

Kalliom held onto her hands. He realized that being there, sharing his work with her, was everything he ever wanted out of a companion.

"I quite enjoy working with you, Kalimon." Haili kissed him on the head and brushed off her robes. "I brought something other than the tart. I will need get it ready in the bedroom."

Kalliom twisted her hands in his and let his heart start to thump heartily. Thankfully, her wine was still untouched.

"Haili," Kalliom said. It was difficult to put into words exactly how he felt for her, but he knew that he wanted her to know that he cared.

Kalliom thought about his employer. *I will convince her.* He simply needed to explain that Haili was more important alive than dead. They would stage an accident and then have her work in secret.

"I do not know how to say this, but I want you to know—"

Haili put a finger over his lips. "Save sentiments for when it matters." She hurried over to the door and grabbed her bag.

Kalliom watched her, feeling a strange measure of contentment.

Haili stopped. "But first, wine." She took a sip of the wine. Her face lit up and she gave him a look that told him it was a treat she did not expect. She picked up the bottle and studied the label. "This is a wonderful gift."

"Just for you," Kalliom said. He could not explain it, but he felt a sadness too deep for words. Maybe he could brew something to slow the process while he worked on an antidote. She had not drunk too much of it. *I can spill the rest on the way to the bedroom.*

Haili lifted the glass to her lips and drank long and deep.

IN DARKNESS
WHITE

JATHALOR STROLLED FORWARD. He looked right and saw nothing but white stretching as far as a distant horizon. To the left was the same. Endless white.

He stopped and tried to decide which direction was west. *I'm good at this.* Unable to make up his mind, Jathalor started to walk in the direction he thought was west. His stomach wasn't rumbling and his head was clear. No need to worry or complain.

Jathalor walked and kept going until he forgot about the concept of time. It felt like the times he strolled with his father during fall among trees colored in shades of fire. No particular direction. No real destination.

How is it possible that I am healthy?

A chilling sensation prickled along his spine. He remembered. They brought him inside a giant cave. He broke free of the man holding him. He ran between giant pillars and rickety wooden structures. He tried climbing and fell.

It was a bad break. It would take a long time to heal.

This, then, was a dream? Jathalor struggled to make sense of it all. His mind warred against itself. Dreams weren't real. They didn't feel real. Jathalor looked down at his legs. He could *feel* them. He walked without pain or weakness, but how was it possible?

A *dream*. He closed his eyes to the endless white. *A lie. Not real, it's not real.*

Jathalor took hold of his strongest memory; one of fishing on the docks of Nathalem with his father.

The day was overcast. Frozen fog made for dim lighting, but the fish never seemed to care much about what was happening above. Bundled in old furs, Jathalor and his father sat watching the water with their poles sticking out of their jackets.

"Not a bad day for fishing," Pa said. "Not bad at all."

"It's cold." Jathalor wiped his runny nose with the back of his hand. "Won't the fish be sleeping?"

"Fish aren't like us, son. They don't worry about when and where. See?" Pointing out to the water, Pa waited until he actually looked before speaking again. "The water's calm. They have no reason to worry, not yet. Wait till the fog clears. Captains will be about their business and these waters will be a mess of waves."

Jathalor buried his face in his jacket and stared at the water gently rolling by. "You'll be sailing soon."

"I'll be back."

"Don't go."

Pa reached over and grabbed Jathalor's shoulder. "I promise to come back for you."

"I don't want you to leave," Jathalor grumbled.

Pa pulled in his line and started to gather the thread for another cast. "There's nothing that can keep me from you."

Jathalor nodded, wiping his runny nose for what felt like the hundredth time.

"Do you believe me?"

Jathalor refused to look at him. "Course, Pa. I know you'll come home."

The memory vanished. The pain in Jathalor's leg prickled and burned. He grimaced at the ache in his knee and ankle. Nothing but darkness, the kind of black that made even a moonless night in the sewers seem bright. Jathalor felt the heat come to his face. Tears followed, spilling from his eyes and snaking down his cheeks.

"PA!" he cried, raw throat burning from the effort. "Pa."

• • •

Taf pushed an aggressive blow to the side, stepped into Braeron's open guard, and smashed his side with the training sword.

Braeron stumbled back, gripping his side. "Depths," he groaned. "There's no need to hit so hard."

"Do we need to take up real blades? Maybe then you will take this seriously."

"It's this useless form you're forcing me into. I've scored against you plenty when I don't have to worry about my feet."

"How many times do I score against you before you manage a lucky hit?"

Braeron stepped toward Taf, his face growing red. "You've years of practice on me."

"Do you think your enemies will care?" Taf hated the arguments from trainees. Always the same, complaining about time or insufficiency. "Learn or die."

"I'm trying."

Taf shook his head disapprovingly. "You are making a mess of your footwork and disregarding my advice."

"Give me room to breathe. Don't have to strike me for every wrong."

"Our enemies will strike us the moment we let down our guard. A snake does not ask to bite you."

"I didn't ask for this, just wanted to learn more blade work."

Taf stepped back, resumed his position, and held his sword at the ready. "You did ask for this."

Braeron was breathing heavily, his chest rising and falling. He gave Taf a look that was very inappropriate for anyone to give their teacher but took his position regardless.

"Start whenever you are ready," Taf said.

Braeron assumed the proper stance, feet apart enough to give stability but not so far as to compromise the need to move. His elbow was held in a position so that his sword could adjust if he needed to be aggressive or defensive.

"Good posture," said Taf.

Braeron did not seem to care for compliments, or criticism for that matter. He was rash, stubborn, and quick with no discipline. He took an aggressive stance that mirrored a well-known stance, but it lacked any kind of polish. He advanced.

Taf blocked the blows as they came, taking a step back and never once compromising the space around him. He controlled where he was and how the battlefield would change. It would make all the difference in a real fight.

Taf side-stepped an attack and knocked the training sword out of Braeron's hand. It was easy. The attack came on the same stride with every step.

"Predictable. You cannot allow me to know where you will strike next."

"Not everyone's as good as you, sir." Braeron picked up his sword.

"You must adjust. Learn or die."

Braeron's mouth twitched as if he were about to speak his mind. Let him say what he would that he might earn some well-deserved chastisement. "Life teaches well enough. Don't need to remind me."

"Do you wish to learn?"

"I'm trying."

"Not well enough."

Braeron tossed the sword to the side. The hardened wood clattered on the ground. "I'm done."

"Typical for a coinsword."

Braeron pulled his right sleeve all the way back and held his forearm out for Taf to see. "I served every year of my term. Stubborn stiff coat." He stormed across the training field and into the compound.

Taf breathed out and forced his hand to let go of the handle of the training sword. The wood hit the ground, sending up a cloud of dust. He massaged his hand to loosen the stiff joints.

He smothered his anger and left the dusty training field for the sanctuary of shade and something cold to drink. In the compound, Arma was waiting for him, a bemused expression on his face.

"He asked for me to teach him," Taf said.

"I have no doubt it was generosity that drove you."

Taf made use of the water basin, drying his clean face with a towel. He twisted his hand the wrong way and felt the joints scream in pain. *I should not lose my temper.*

"It would help if he gave an honest effort," said Taf. "I have no need to waste my time with him."

"You know," Arma said, "I think I recall someone else young, talented, who was prone to lose their temper. From what I remember, they hated drills of any kind."

Taf snorted. "Still do."

Arma held up a roll of paper.

"Maps?"

"Yes. Arrived from Nathalem just this morning."

"That was faster than I thought." Taf wrestled with asking what he really wanted to know. "Any other news?"

Arma spread the map out on the small desk and placed a dagger on one corner and his coin purse on the other side. "You mean from your mistress?"

"She is not my mistress."

"He still has his temper."

Taf felt the heat in his face and took several deep breaths to distill his frustration.

Arma produced a small envelope and handed it to Taf. "I only read the first three lines. It was enough to make me uncomfortable."

Taf snatched the letter and checked. The seam was unbroken. He whipped out his dagger and ran it across the edge of the envelope to the sound of hissing paper.

He walked away from Arma who strained to look over his shoulder. The first few lines were updates on policies they had worked to write together. The middle confirmed what he needed to know. The last lines stopped him. *I have forgotten what it means to be apart. To say I miss you is an understatement. It is as if a part of me is without. How did we ever drift? I should have stayed and fought for you. A lesson I will not soon forget.*

"I have received word from the Shadows," said Arma. He was staring down at the map which proved to be a detailed rendering of the whole island of Telem.

Taf stepped up the table. "Can they confirm Braeron's word?"

"No one within the Board of Masters suspects this Kalliom or anyone else. Our contact has only been able to confirm that the Briars are on location."

"That is enough to convince me to set sail. Who knows how long Jathalor has."

Arma did not say anything, but Taf knew what he was thinking. It was probably already too late. Regardless, they needed to stop whatever was happening. That was the King's primary concern.

"What do we know?" asked Taf, studying the massive library that took up most of the island. Where would anyone hide captives? From what he understood, the entire library was used. Even the more obscure archives were at least cleaned regularly.

"The most recent report confirms the location," said Arma. "The Shadow recently discovered a trading barge with several cells in the cargo hold. We still have no idea where the prisoners are transported to once they arrive."

"That is unhelpful."

Arma nodded and pointed to large entrances within the library. "These are doors that lead to a lower level. There are no clear locks."

"A secret underground system beneath the most reputable learning institution in the world. We would need to convince the Board to let us have access."

Arma looked up at Taf. "The Council does not know how the doors work."

Taf let the news settle in. "How is that possible?"

"The doors are remnants from the castle that used to reside on Telem."

"From before the Sundering?"

"That is what the Shadow was told. Repeatedly. No one even seems bothered. The Shadow even checked to see if they could find the entrance points around the island, but they found nothing."

Taf set both hands on the table and leaned in hard. "We have a course to set and no direction."

"I have a few ideas," said Arma.

"Any of them good?" Taf asked.

"Hard to say."

Taf needed to find that boy. *Be alive.* Jatha, the boy's father, was waiting on the ship with the rest of the crew. He was insistent on knowing everything he was allowed, but Taf was starting to worry Jatha would ask the one question Taf did not have an answer for. Would they want to find him, or what was left of him?

"I will take a course over nothing at all." Taf tucked the folded letter into his shirt. "We leave as soon as we can. I will make sure the brat knows."

· · ·

Darkness, it was all around him. Cold, the constant touch of metal.

The man in robes would come; he always did. He spoke of strange things with a woman who sounded nice but did nothing

162

to stop the robed man. He would force Jathalor to drink some tincture that tasted of bitter chalk. Then came the White.

Jathalor shifted his weight just enough to relieve the pressure on his broken leg. His stomach protested the gnawing emptiness. His dry throat made it painful to take a full breath. He thought about a drink of cool water, the sweet relief as it trickled down his throat.

I'm alive. When he felt his broken leg and empty stomach, he knew he wasn't in the White. Was pain his only comfort now?

Death lingered as the final end to his captivity. It wasn't something he worried about. Why would he? He'd no choice now. There was only one way his story ended.

That was why he hated hearing the key working inside the lock. If the door opened, then the man in dark robes would come and the White soon after. He was starting to think the White was worse than death. He felt his body suspended in the White, a prison built of lies, and trembled.

The sound of steps echoing off stone came from the hall-way. The key slid into the lock. Metal scraped against metal, ending in a soft click. Jathalor closed his eyes. The door creaked open.

• • •

Taf paced the deck of the *King's Herald* long after nightfall. The craft glided across the waters at a good pace, the strong head-wind they picked up during the afternoon guiding them toward Telem. They would be there faster than he had expected. *Not fast enough.*

He walked beside the railing, feeling the gentle rock of the ship moving to and fro. Exhaustion clung to the edges of his mind. He should be sleeping, but when he laid down his mind raced. If he walked long enough, maybe his body would just collapse.

The boy was suffering. Either he was caged or dead. Neither was an option he could let sit in his stomach.

The haunted memories of his past infected his worries. His father was never home, always found in a bad state after having drunk too much or done something foolish at work. Taf bore the weight of his distant, abusive father until he did what only seemed right. He ran. Away from a mother and a sister who needed him.

By the time he went home there was nothing to be found. His father was dead, mother and sister gone. For all his searching, he could never find them. His best hope was they had both found something, anything, better.

This boy was loved. Despite no mother to help and a life working for scraps, Jathalor's father was willing to risk everything to find him. It hurt. He thought that hole in his heart was buried with the bones of the past.

I will find Jathalor. It was hope. A good and honest bearing to carry him away from sorrow that could never be changed.

Taf fingered the coin in his pocket and thought about the Camoor he helped. That boy was one of many suffering, and he was glad to live a life where he could give what he had in service of those less fortunate. The past remained a bitter memory, but the future was yet unwritten.

He found himself at the door to his cabin. Taf threw it open, the wood slamming on the wall. A loud thud sounded from the corner where Braeron had fallen out of his hammock. Taf smiled to himself.

"Any luck?" asked Taf.

Arma was sitting at a table poring over maps and charts. In the far corner, Braeron cursed and grumbled his way back into bed.

Arma raised an eyebrow. "If you expect divine revelation, I recommend talking to a priest. I could write the High Father back in Nathalem."

"I have no use for religion now."

Arma leaned back in his chair. "As far as I can determine, we have three courses of action. We can appeal to the Board. I sent word earlier asking that a meeting be set up with all haste. There is the option of distracting the Thow while one of us attempts to open one of the doors. And lastly, we can appeal to the King for a Writ of Search."

"Lady Maisali said that relations with the Thow are not as stable as we hoped. The King may not be comfortable conceding to such drastic measures." Taf laid both hands on the table and stared at the map he knew by heart. What was he missing?

"There's always another way in," said Braeron.

Taf pushed down the immediate anger that rose in his chest. The training session that morning had been disastrous. Not only did Braeron not listen, but he constantly complained. *If he calls me stiff coat one more time...*

Braeron walked over to the table and yawned, stretching. His breath was awful.

"No one asked your opinion," Taf said.

Arma leaned back in his chair. "No man's a fool who can listen rather than speak."

Taf shot Arma a bitter look.

Braeron, seemingly oblivious, leaned on the table with both arms outstretched. "The doors aren't exactly the easy option. There's got to be something. A secret passage? Break through a weak part in the floor?"

"They sneak the passengers at night around the far side of the Library," said Taf, "but we have no idea how they get in. Even the Shadow has yet to determine the entrance."

"Shadow?" asked Braeron. "What kind of shadow we talking about?"

Arma smiled, obviously pleased that the King's secret hand was not even a rumor among a man who served in the military. "You will know when you meet them."

"So it's a person, or someone. Something?"

Taf looked over at Braeron. "How would you get in?"

"Have them take me captive. Then I'd know how to get in and out."

Arma and Taf exchanged a hopeful glance. Braeron caught on quickly enough to cross his arms. "Isn't a way in the depths I'm doing that. Spent enough time in the Briar's brambles already."

It might work. It made sense. "Jatha," Taf said.

Arma nodded his agreement. "I will send word now."

• • •

Jathalor ran as fast as his legs could carry him. Like a great sail caught by a powerful wind, he felt no need to stop, no need to breathe. He felt as if he could lift off the ground and soar into the endless White above him.

A gnawing sensation in the back of his mind kept him from enjoying his freedom. Jathalor slowed his pace until he came to a complete stop. Something was wrong, but he could not explain it. He closed his eyes. Jathalor tried to anchor his thoughts. Nothing was different, just the same White, and yet he could feel it closing in like a blanket around him. He dropped to his knees and put his hands over his head.

"Rise," called a voice, clear and sinister.

Jathalor slowly lifted his eyes. A figured, shaped like a man, stood before him, tall and menacing. The phantom glowed white. Tendrils like flame danced on the edge of the figure's outline.

"I demand that you rise." The phantom reached out a hand toward Jathalor.

The pressure doubled its force. Discomfort twisted into unexpected pain. Jathalor pushed one leg off the ground and started to stand.

Anchor. When a ship was off the dock its only hope of staying grounded was the anchor. He needed something to hold him, anything to keep him from drifting.

He grabbed the memory he had used as an anchor before. Jathalor recalled every detail he could. The smell of the salty water. The sound of his father's voice cutting through the foggy morning.

Jathalor stayed anchored on the dock, cold wind against his face, his father only a few feet away. The longer he waited, the less the White held to him.

"Do you believe me, son?" Pa asked.

"I do," Jathalor told him. He forced the words through the White and its binding emptiness. "I do."

• • •

Taf waited with Braeron at the far end of the dock. In the distance he could see the *King's Herald* alight and busy with the work of loading and unloading supplies.

"Not one for waiting," said Braeron. "Gets my nerves to jumping."

Taf bit back a reprimand. "I want to get to knocking a few heads."

"I'm the same. Can't stop thinking about the boy. Been worse since we landed. I let him go to the captain without a thought otherwise."

Taf found himself humbled by the admission. Of course he was not the only one who cared. It was so easy to get lost in his own head.

"You would have fought for him if you knew," Taf said. It was supposed to sound more comforting than it came across.

"I'm going to fight tonight."

Arma emerged from the shadows. "The distraction is in place. The captain has a few of the Board members preparing a last-minute meal for us."

"A good ruse," said Taf. "How long do we need to wait on the Shadow?"

Arma did not say a word but looked behind Taf.

Taf knew the answer the moment he asked the question. "They are already here."

Taf turned to see the Shadow standing behind them. Despite being on edge and awaiting word, Taf had heard nothing of the

Shadow's coming. They were dressed in all black, melding perfectly with the dark. All Taf could see were the eyes peering under
the hood. The Shadow's face was masked by a featureless metal
piece that fit perfectly from cheek to chin.

A blade flashed in the dim light. The Shadow held the
short sword to Braeron's throat. Unlike traditional weapons, the
Shadow's blade came to a squared edge. From what Taf knew, the
edge was so sharp it could cut a feather that fell onto it.

"Who?" asked the Shadow.

"A temporary hand," Arma said. "You have permission to
sever if the need arises."

The Shadow stepped up to Braeron, their arm holding the
blade in perfect stillness while they moved. They eyed Braeron
long enough to make Taf worried about the boy's neck.

The blade vanished as quickly as it came. The Shadow moved
across the deck to the furthest end. Arma led the trio over to
where the Shadow stood sentinel.

Arma stepped into the water. Taf nearly lurched to grab him,
but his friend did not sink.

Taf caught a glimpse of the boat, if that was the right word.
It went down instead of up but looked to be nearly as large as a
five-man rower. The edges sat on top of the water, but that was all
he could see.

"I am not getting in that," said Taf.

Arma turned around, already halfway submerged. "There
is nothing to fret over. The Kingdom has used these for several
years now."

"Wearing full plate and being on a ship is foolish enough.
You are asking me to go into the water."

"I don't swim well," Braeron said, almost as if to himself.

Arma vanished.

"Our quarry is on the move," said the Shadow.

Braeron passed Taf and headed down, testing the first step before clambering down. He could hear the conversation at his funeral now. *How did Taf die? Wearing full plate at sea.* Not exactly a noble way to be remembered.

Taf headed into the depths. It was dark and damp but did not smell of mold. He was surprised to find the bottom of the ship was dry. He tested the walls with his hand and found that they were not soaked or leaking.

A figure slid past him. No matter how many times he had worked with Shadows, the feeling of being in their presence left him unnerved. If rumors were to be believed, Lady Maisali had started her career as a Shadow. Politician by day, assassin by night. His thoughts drifted to inappropriate places, and he reined them back in.

"Oars," said Arma.

Taf settled into the furthest position and took up the oars on either side. He could hear Braeron fumbling about with his.

"Sit this out," said Taf. "Having one less oar is better than having one working against."

Braeron mumbled something about wanting to help. Taf felt the craft start to move and joined Arma, falling into perfect rhythm. Years and dozens of battles could have that effect on people.

Taf felt better as they cruised along. He still had many questions about how the vessel did not sink and how the Shadow knew where to go, but these were unimportant. They were on their way.

Jatha had been more than willing and the Briars took the bait.

Arma slowed his pace, and Taf muscled his oars to match tempo. They hit a crawl. Were they finally sinking?

Taf listened to the strange sound of the ship, wondering all the while what in Ta'Thaloon was happening. The ship lurched and he grabbed his seat.

The Shadow moved. Taf counted the movement, pacing out how much distance they typically traveled. If he needed to, he could at least manage a hit on the Shadow.

Taf gladly headed up the stairs, breathing deeply the salty air. His thoughts snapped into focus when he saw what was happening. The wall of stone in front of them was moving.

Huge chunks of rock and vegetation were shifting to either side to make room for several small rowboats getting ready to deposit their prisoners. Taf could see Jatha on the second boat, tied up, face illuminated by the light pouring out of the opening.

The Shadow crouched on the edge of the boat. He caught sight of her figure, slender neck, and black, braided hair.

The Shadow leapt a seemingly impossible distance and entered the water without a splash. Taf watched to see where she was going. He never saw her emerge, but he watched a rope attached to the front of the craft snap taut.

The ship started to move. His fear that the craft would take on water quickly vanished as he noticed them heading toward the opening and the extended plank where the other ships were unloading.

Taf felt his heart start to beat to the rhythm of battle. He lowered himself and stretched out his arms. Arma undid something and pulled back part of the ship so that Braeron and he could join him.

"Does not look like we will have much time," said Arma.

Taf watched as the prisoner drop quickly came to an end.

"Might need to make a dramatic entrance," Taf said.

"Heroics are not always the best option."

"Any other ideas?"

Arma watched as they drew within spitting distance of the entrance. He breathed out. "Heroics it is."

"Never thought I'd be wrecking about a Briar's den," said Braeron. "Not again."

Taf unhitched his helmet from his belt and slid it onto his head, smiling. "Come now. This is the fun part."

Taf leapt out of the boat and landed on the deck. He slid his sword free while charging headlong at three Briars. The men fumbled to do anything.

Taf cut the first thug across the chest and drove his blade into the next Briar's stomach. He slid his sword free, driving his momentum to the side and using the force to send the last man to the ground whimpering.

Arma killed a Briar and pushed the man onto the mechanism holding the door open. The chains yanked and pulled to a stop.

Braeron charged past Taf and engaged a Briar. The enemy was ready, sword in hand and stance set. Taf wondered if this would be Braeron's last dance.

Braeron pushed the man back with stunningly precise blows that eventually opened the Briar's guard. Braeron stabbed the man in the gut before shoving him over and moving toward two Briars still struggling to get their bearings.

Taf turned around, remembering the ships with their crews. An arrow to the back would not be fun, even with plate. The closest boat was the only one with anyone on it. The Shadow emerged from the water and ended the two remaining Briars before diving off the edge and vanishing into the murky depths.

Taf jogged to catch up with Arma. The Briars were retreating farther into the depths of their hideout. The place looked like it had once been catacombs. Huge statues lined the walls. Crumbling pillars with faded designs ran the length of the room. The Briars had constructed a patchwork framework of wood with several cages lining either side of the wall.

He glanced over at Braeron. He did not need any help. One of the Briars was already lying in a pool of blood, the other limping away. *I misjudged him.* It was a bitter thought. Taf should have known better than to think Braeron a liar.

Taf cut loose the bindings holding Jatha. "Let us be about freeing these people. We will find your son."

• • •

Jathalor lay face down on the White. Summoning his resolve, he threw his elbow forward and dragged the rest of his body.

The phantom stood beside him, a wicked effigy of flaming white.

"Resistance will cost you everything," the figure told him.

Jathalor could feel himself becoming less, like he was a cracked jar constantly leaking water.

The phantom bent over and pressed its hand on Jathalor's back. Pain like a burning coal spread over him. He gripped both hands and gritted his teeth.

"Submit to my will."

Jathalor pushed off with his knees.

"Stop."

Jathalor lost control of his body. He slumped onto the White, useless and empty.

"You will surrender to me."

"I will."

"Give yourself to me. Swear on your name."

Jathalor felt himself speak. "I…"

"Give yourself."

"I, Jathalor, give—"

He remembered his father and he knew his father loved him.

"I. Will. Not." The numbing started to give way to the pain of his broken leg and the discomfort of the metal table he lay on. He didn't like the ache and throb of his body, but it was real, real enough to keep the White away. Jathalor focused on the pain.

He felt the White receding, the pain coming forward. Suddenly he was back in the darkness. Jathalor strained forward, his head rising no higher than his chest before he slumped back on the table. His chest rose and fell with a heavy breath.

The robed man broke the silence. "What gives you so much strength? How is it you defy me? You are nothing. Even if you survive, the life that awaits you is destined to be filled with pain and disappointment. You will work until you die. Family members will die if disease and hardship do not take them first.

"This is better. What I offer you is rest. No more pain, no more fear. To think you could be free from all the terrible worries of this life. Submit to me. Say you will, and I will make everything better."

A silence filled the darkness of the room. Jathalor felt himself slipping into weariness. He needed to pay attention; his father once told him knowledge was one of the strongest weapons a man could wield.

"A Camoor with a will, what a strange roadblock. I will give you one more dose, and if you resist me again, I will kill you with my own hands. If only for the satisfaction."

Jathalor passed out.

· · ·

Taf charged forward with Braeron and Arma beside him.

Taf parried a man and let Arma gut him. Braeron pushed one of the Briars back, giving Taf the chance to slice through the man's sword arm. Arma blocked an attack headed for Taf. Braeron gutted the Briar before he could get his guard up.

The remaining Briars retreated. Taf led them farther into the catacombs. Tombs dedicated to long-dead kings were broken and abandoned. The rows of burial beds held skeletons and mummified remains barely visible in the dim light of abandoned torches and hanging lanterns.

So far, they had found only empty cages. Find the Thow responsible. It made the most sense. Hopefully, they did not have enough time to get away. Hopefully, there were more prisoners.

Ahead of them a barricade of wood blocked their passage.

"Arrows," Taf shouted.

The trio ducked out of the way behind a giant pillar.

"How long have they been working down here?" asked Taf. "How did we not know the Briars were so fortified?"

"I am starting to think we know a lot less than we hoped," Arma said.

"Any thoughts?"

Braeron peeked around the corner. "That gate doesn't look too weak. A battering ram would be nice."

Arma tapped his shoulder twice. Taf was not one to argue on the battlefield, but rushing a gate without a shield or allies to shoot at the archers seemed a fool's errand.

Arma moved out of cover and headed right for the gate. Taf followed with Braeron cursing while he took up the rear.

The archers on the right stopped shooting. A lucky shot struck Taf in the shoulder, bouncing off with a soft clang. *Thank the stars for plate.*

The archers on the left stopped, and then there was silence. Arma stood in front of the gate, breathing heavily and looking up to the top of the wooden mess of stacked boards.

"How many do you think will be waiting for us?" Braeron asked, coming alongside the two of them.

"Not enough," said Taf.

The gate groaned and creaked until it swung open. The Briars charged.

Taf met the oncoming rush with Arma beside him. He cut down the first Briar with ease, engaging another wielding a spiked club while worried about the three taking position on his right flank. Braeron slew one of the thugs and closed the gap.

Arma danced with three men, avoiding a spear and slashing a man across the neck before elbowing the next man. He twisted in a circle and brought his blade down on the next man.

Taf stabbed a man in the arm and adjusted to an incoming spear. The edge struck his plate and made a screech as it slid across the metal. Braeron brought his weapon down on the shaft of the spear. Taf danced around Braeron and cut down a Briar about to attack.

Braeron matched Taf's tempo. They fought back-to-back, twisting and turning to keep their enemies constantly guessing who was going to strike next. The dead multiplied.

Arma bulled over a Briar and drove him through.

"We need to pull back," said Arma.

Taf could see the remaining Briars starting to close in. All three backed away with swords held at the ready. A large man wearing plate and wielding a huge axe stepped out of the crowd.

"That one is mine," said Taf.

A blast of powder exploded between Taf and the big man. Smoke started to crawl across the floor creating a gray cloud that blanketed the battlefield in obscurity. Taf kept his guard up and advanced in the direction of the massive Briar.

He followed the heavy tread of boots. He saw the large shadow taking form in the midst of the field of gray. A huge axe came down in front of Taf.

He moved to the side, avoiding a wild swing. He attacked, hitting armor, and adjusted. The axe flew overhead. He stepped close and rammed his sword into the exposed leg. A backhand sent him stumbling back, disarmed.

He hit the ground hard. *How strong—* He rolled away. The axe slammed into the stone where Taf had just been, chipping the stone.

He grasped the handle of his blade with both hands and pulled. The weapon slid out of the Briar's leg. Taf drove the blade through the leather covering the Briar's midsection. The blade went all the way through. The large axe clattered to the ground.

The smoke began to disseminate. Braeron and Arma were beating back a group of Briars who looked to be about to break. Toward the edge of the conflict, a figure darted about, cutting down unsuspecting Briars. Taf slid his sword free of the dying man and held it at the ready. Crimson flowed down his blade, dripping off the edge lazily.

The battle felt on the verge of turning. Taf started jogging until he was thundering toward the enemy. Adrenaline filled the spaces left by exhaustion. He cut down one after another until the few Briars not writhing in their blood were tripping their way in a hasty, disorganized retreat. They would find no relief in the shadows.

"We've ground to cover yet," said Braeron. He had that look in his eyes men got whenever the battle turned in their favor and killing had not yet settled uncomfortably. "Jathalor will be saved."

Taf followed Arma and Braeron as they passed through the open gate and away from the field of corpses. The Briars' compound was larger than Taf had thought.

The occasional corpse littered the hauntingly empty hideout. Only once did he catch glimpse of the Shadow. A thought came to mind, and the fact it only happened now left him feeling more bothered than it might have otherwise. Why would the King invest so much manpower into a rescue? Yes, kidnapping within the Kingdom troubled everyone, but there were always other matters of state to be attended to.

The vast, empty catacombs began to tighten until they were faced with a set of stairs that headed up into a corridor shrouded by shadow. Braeron turned around and headed back toward the compound, probably to find a light source.

The Shadow stood right behind them holding out two lanterns. "Thanks," Braeron said, nearly dropping the lantern during the exchange.

The Shadow followed them as Braeron boldly led them up the stairs. An odd sensation haunted the cramped stairway. As they left the stairs and walked into a room that looked like it may have served as a religious site, the feeling only got worse. Whatever was happening here was more significant than he had realized.

They left the room and entered another hallway that split to the right and left.

"It is hard to believe the Thow do not know about this," Taf said. Or maybe they did not want to acknowledge it.

"Go right," said the Shadow.

Taf wanted to know how she knew, but Braeron surged ahead with the lantern sending the darkness into full retreat.

The unsettling feeling grew until Taf needed to take a deep breath to still his roiling stomach.

Arma looked over at him, obviously puzzled.

A childhood tale came to mind wherein a small boy and girl left home despite their parents' warning and found themselves in trouble with an unsavory character. He felt the need to speak wisdom from the fable.

"Wickedness wanders within or without, and I wonder the way." As if to validate his concerns, the light from Braeron's torch revealed a cart with several bodies stacked atop each other.

"Not right," Braeron said, his voice trembling. "I swear on the stars that worm'll pay for this."

Taf was in full agreement.

The smooth walls of the tunnel gave way to several doors. They were bolted shut. The Shadow pressed her ear against the closest one.

"Breathing."

At the next room she said nothing, and the silence told him enough. Taf felt the roiling in his gut starting to reach a gnawing frustration. They would need a key to check the rooms, and the Thow probably kept it. Did they already pass Jathalor? Was there even the sound of breathing coming from his room?

The Shadow darted forward, melting into the darkness. The trio hurried to keep pace. The thunder of boots clanged off the walls. If there was any hope of a surprise it was long lost.

The light illuminated a door slightly ajar. Taf surged past his friends, grabbed the door, and swung the heavy metal frame like it was a stick tossed to the side. He stormed into the room.

A robed man sat with his back to the door. A young Camoor lay strapped to a table in front of him, illuminated by candlelight. Words were uttered. They were coarse and evil but whispered soft enough to be meant for a lover.

Taf placed the edge of his sword against Kalliom's throat. That got the man's attention. The sudden stop of the wicked words lifted the strange sensation. The boy on the table jerked to life.

"Kalliom, is it? Stand," Taf commanded.

The Thow slowly rose. "I suppose we are past formal introductions."

"Braeron, bind his hands."

While Braeron worked securing the Thow, Arma started to help the boy.

"Pa?" the boy asked weakly.

Arma held the boy's hand and gently coaxed him to a seated position. Taf stepped up to the table. "Jathalor?"

The boy looked up at him. "Pa?"

Taf turned to Arma. "Best to get the father. We have no notion as to the damage that has been done."

The Shadow and Arma headed back the way they came. Taf kept the boy steady. His eyes were bloodshot, and the hue of his skin appeared sickly, almost gray.

"Did you even feed them?" asked Taf.

"Of course, I fed them," Kalliom said. "I needed them alive. Did I not?"

"I've no notion of what you've done," said Braeron. "But I know you didn't care to keep them alive. The dead speak to your crimes."

Kalliom chuckled. "Crimes indeed. Typical for a Katal. So worried about honor that you cannot allow yourself to even imagine what good might come from what I am doing here."

"Keep him quiet," Taf said. "He can give us his grand speech when he sits before the throne awaiting execution."

That kept the Thow silent. The sound of boots coming down the hallway ended with Jatha, led by the Shadow, bursting into the room and gathering his son in his arms. The look on their faces, the warmth of reunion. It was almost too much for Taf. He slipped out and took a long, deep breath that he let out slowly.

The Shadow joined Taf in the hall, lantern in one hand. She dipped her head respectfully. "I will secure the way back. King and Kingdom."

"King and Kingdom." Those words tasted justified.

Taf felt a comfortable warmth ease the pain in his joints from so much running. He was not as young as he used to be. Thoughts rolled over the past few days. *I owe Braeron an apology.* How had he been so harsh?

Harsh, wicked words shattered the peace. Taf hurried into the room. Braeron was already ahead of him, hand clamped onto the Thow's mouth.

"He's trying something awful," said Braeron.

"Keep him silent. Arma, escort the boy back. I assume our reinforcements will be waiting for us by now."

Jatha carried Jathalor out of the room and into the hallway. Taf stayed one step behind the Thow, blade pressed into the small of his back. It felt as if something in the shadows were stalking them, ready to pounce.

"Ow!" Braeron cried, drawing back his hand now bleeding.

Kalliom screamed several words. Taf drove his blade into the Thow's back, the wicked speech ending with a whimper of pain. Kalliom collapsed and the tunnel started to rumble.

A door ahead of them creaked open. A single figure stepped out into the flickering light. What had once been a person was now a twisted mess of metal and gray flesh. The eyes that stared forward were white and empty. On each arm a single length of sharpened steel jutted out like talons.

Kalliom spoke again before slumping to the floor.

The sound of metal clinking on the floor bounced off the stone walls from behind and before. Taf turned to cover their backs. Three of the figures were approaching.

"Sever the limbs," Arma said, his voice carrying an edge only battle provoked. "Arms first."

Taf leapt into action. He cut the first monstrosity's right

arm and dodged a swipe coming for his midsection. He severed another limb and then another. They were slow.

A talon passed by his face. Not as slow as he assumed. Taf slashed an arm, then a leg, and left the last monstrosity limping backwards until it collapsed.

The room across from where they found Jathalor was now open. A monstrosity stepped toward the two Camoor. Jatha stumbled as he tried to carry his son to safety. Taf reached them just in time to knock the talon out of the way. He sliced off the right arm while Braeron sliced off the left.

Kalliom started to laugh. The sound was pained and garbled but cruel nonetheless. "Katal and their honor. You say you are willing to fight. King and Kingdom." The words were distastefully said. Kalliom propped himself up on his elbow. "Tell me, what is the life of a Camoor actually worth? A sixth of a Katal?"

Taf lowered his blade to Kalliom's face. "A life for a life."

"Prove it," Kalliom spat. He spoke three wicked words and vanished in a cloud of smoke.

Jathalor began to scream. One of the metal bindings still attached to the boy's ankle glowed as if it had just been forged. Taf dropped to his knees and grabbed the shackle with both hands. He strained to pull the binding apart.

He connected with Jathalor. A tether of palpable energy anchored them to each other. Taf did not understand how or why it was happening, but he knew the cost. Kalliom was draining Jathalor to fuel his cruel deception. The boy's life force faded like a candle about to burn out.

Taf decided to take the pain. The drain was instantaneous. It felt as if hot coals were being shoved down his throat and pushed into every part of his body. Every heartbeat pushed him one step closer to a ravenous darkness.

Let go. It was a simple idea and one he knew he could accomplish. If only he let go for a moment and split the burden with Jathalor, Taf felt he could endure. But he knew the boy's life was closer to the darkness than his own. Taf closed his eyes and shouldered the weight.

The burning ended with a sudden chill that left Taf shivering. He fell onto the ground. There should have been pain from hitting his shoulder, but the world was a haze.

Arma knelt in front of him, helping him to sit up against the wall. "Look here," he said. "Taf, look me in the eyes. Deep breaths."

Taf met Arma's gaze, and the truth became strikingly clear. There was no fear, only sorrow. Taf let the sadness settle deep inside his heart. It was right and good.

"Thank you," Taf said. He coughed, the taste of ash clogging his nose and mouth.

"They have been good years. Great years, even."

Taf tried to speak again but found the words drifting just out of reach. "Lady Maisali," he said. A memory of their last night came to mind and it cleared away all the pain.

"I will carry the word myself."

Taf looked past Arma to Braeron who was standing with his sword held properly and his eyes wide. "Come," he told the young man.

Braeron approached, obviously uneasy.

Taf picked up his sword, slowly turned it around, and held it handle-first to Braeron. "A gift from the King," Taf told him. "I give it to you under vow."

Braeron sheathed his own sword and wrapped a trembling

hand around the handle. "What am I to swear?"

"King and Kingdom. You have a good heart, Braeron."

"King and Kingdom," Braeron echoed. As the blade slid out of Taf's hand, he grabbed the metal. Blood oozed from his hands.

"Swear it."

Braeron stared down at the crimson dripping off the blade. "King and Kingdom." The words were spoken with heart and that was enough.

Taf looked over at the two Camoor, a father and son reunited. "Jathalor."

Jatha propped up his son and held his head upright. The boy still looked as if he were elsewhere. Taf fished in his pocket with fingers that felt almost like they belonged to someone else. He fumbled to hold onto the coin as he drew it out. He took Jathalor's hand and placed the silver in his palm, wrapping the fingers over the gift.

Taf tried to speak. It was as if he knew the right words for what happened but could not find them. Everything was starting to grow dim and distant. Memories muddled and thoughts drifted.

"Live," Taf said, squeezing the boy's hand.

The boy tilted his head to the side and looked Taf in the eyes.

"It is all I ask." The numbing emptiness crawled over him until it swallowed him whole.

• • •

Kalliom chuckled to himself. The foolish Katal had taken his bait perfectly, sacrificing himself and ensuring the energy did not cost any of Kalliom's own life. Kalliom worked the metallic taste around his mouth and swallowed some spit, but the bitter reminder of the magic lingered regardless. Science was a much more stable means of accomplishing his ends, but he would not deny that magic could be useful.

He pulled the firestone from inside his robes and rolled it around his palm while whispering the forbidden words. The embers within the dark gemstone blazed into a warm glow. The light illuminated the hallways. His study should only be a short walk ahead. Blasted tunnels all started to look the same.

The wound screamed in his back, stinging with every step. Kalliom focused on making careful steps. He could patch himself easily enough once he made it to his study.

He leaned against the wall and took a moment to breathe through his teeth. The shadows parted to reveal a figure standing in the hallway watching him.

"Oh good," Kalliom said, feeling elated. "Stupid Katal just had to go and stab me. A shame he is too dead to savor my pain."

The woman stayed perfectly still. Her eyes caught the red glow from his firestone producing a strange glare.

"Well then?" asked Kalliom. "Will you not help me? My study is only a bit farther."

"I am not here to help you," the woman said. Her words seeped into his bones and sent a chill up his spine.

"I may not yet be dead, but I am wounded. You must help me. I require it."

The woman smiled. "No."

"How dare you," Kalliom growled, trying to push forward but finding the pain too much to bear. "I have done all that you have asked. Given more time I will be able to create an army more terrifying than anything this world has ever seen. You need me."

"Do I?" she asked, tilting her head to the side.

Another figure emerged from the darkness. Kalliom recognized her at once, for length of time spent and the fondness of memories were not so easy distilled.

"Haili?" asked Kalliom. A joy filled his heart to the brim. "I thought you were dead. I touched your cold face."

"Did you find everything," the woman asked Haili.

"Everything." Haili carried several books, all of which Kalliom knew because he had written them. She was holding his entire life's work.

Anger overcame the momentary joy. "What is the meaning of this? I did all that you asked. If you want a war—"

She laughed, and it was the cruelest sound Kalliom had ever heard. "I could buy an army, I can start a war. These are simple matters and truthfully, men tend to incite their own destruction regardless of my intervention."

Kalliom felt a sudden lightheadedness. He needed to get to his study. He took a feeble step forward and collapsed.

Footsteps approached. The woman knelt down and leaned in close so that Kalliom could smell the dense fragrance of her perfume.

"I do not want war," she whispered. "Why would I waste time building an army to destroy the world? The fabric of peace is already tearing, and what do you think will happen when trust and stability are replaced by fear and doubt? For all your intelligence you lack clarity. You poor fool. I want something so much better than war. I want to watch Ta'Thaloon tear itself to pieces."

EPILOGUE

JALI WATCHED the dying embers of the fire. An occasional pop sounded from the charred husks of wood.

"I'd not asked for a sad story," she said.

Jaja reached over and squeezed her hand. "Most stories are a little sad."

Jali glanced over at her parents' door.

Jaja yawned loudly and turned over, snuggling against the chair.

"Jaja," Jali said softly.

"Hmm?"

"That's not the end, is it?"

Jaja snored loudly.

Jali stood up and shook her grandfather, who started chuckling. "No. That's not the end."

TO BE CONTINUED...

There is much more to Ta'Thaloon and much more to this tale. Look for book II, SACRIFICE, in late 2021.

ABOUT THE AUTHOR

CHRISTOPHER WOLFE is a quirky, caffeine dependent human being driven by ambition and tempered by the loving support of great family and friends. He writes fantasy novels spawned from the deep recess of his imagination and includes the bits of wisdom he has found along the way.

Currently living in Mississippi, Christopher manages a local restaurant. When he is not living everyday life as a husband and father, he spends time lifting heavy things, reading an assortment of genres, and conquering worlds via videogames.

Connect with Christopher at his website:
mcpherrenwriting.com

or via Facebook:
@AuthorChristopherWolfe

www.ingramcontent.com/pod-product-compliance
Lightning Source LLC
Chambersburg PA
CBHW022151240626
47153CB00007B/2608